DISCARD

MISADVENTURES
ON THE
REBOUND

BY
LAUREN ROWE

PALM BEACH COUNTY
LIBRARY SYSTEM
3650 Summit Boulevard
West Palm Beach, FL 33406-4198

MISADVENTURES
ON THE
REBOUND

BY
LAUREN ROWE

WATERHOUSE PRESS

This book is an original publication of Waterhouse Press.

This is a work of fiction. Names, characters, places, and incidents either are the product of the author's imagination or are used fictitiously, and any resemblance to actual persons, living or dead, business establishments, events, or locales is entirely coincidental. The publisher does not assume any responsibility for third-party websites or their content.

Copyright © 2018 Waterhouse Press, LLC
Cover Design by Waterhouse Press.
Cover images: Shutterstock

All Rights Reserved.
No part of this book may be reproduced, scanned, or distributed in any printed or electronic format without permission. Please do not participate in or encourage piracy of copyrighted materials in violation of the author's rights. Purchase only authorized editions.

PRINTED IN THE UNITED STATES OF AMERICA

ISBN: 978-1-64263-010-7

To Dad. I'm awfully glad I've got a great one.

PROLOGUE

SAVANNAH

Las Vegas, Nevada

Five and a half years ago

My heart thudding in my ears, I walk slowly down the hallway of my high school toward him. *Mason Crenshaw.* His back is to me. His muscular, beautiful, captain-of-the-football-team back. The back I gripped on Saturday night when I unexpectedly lost my virginity to him at a Halloween party. In a closet. While dressed like a chicken. But I try not to think about that last detail. Pretend I never mentioned the chicken part.

Mason Crenshaw.

The gorgeous boy I've had a crush on since fourth grade but hadn't uttered a single word to until two weeks ago. That's when my multi-variable calculus teacher asked me to tutor Mason in basic algebra because he'd been offered a full-ride football scholarship to UNLV. "But he won't be going anywhere on scholarship—not UNLV or clown college—if he can't pass algebra," my teacher explained. And now, just two weeks after uttering my first algebra-induced word to Mason, he's no longer my secret crush with whom I've never spoken. He's the boy who unexpectedly pocketed my virginity on Saturday night.

I wasn't even supposed to go to that Halloween party. I only went because my next-door neighbor and lifelong best friend, Kyle, dragged me there. Apparently, one of the football players is secretly gay and had invited Kyle to the party. "Bring a fake date or don't show up at all," the guy told Kyle. So, yeah, I finally attended my first "cool kid" party during my senior year of high school...as my gay next-door neighbor's beard while dressed as fowl.

And guess what crazy, unexpected factoid I discovered the moment I walked into that party. Cool-kid high school girls don't dress like egg-layers for Halloween. Nope. They dress like sexy French maids and naughty nurses and Catholic schoolgirls gone awry. There wasn't a hen or turkey or even a peacock to be found. And that made sense to me, actually, once I thought about it. Popular girls like Amanda Silvestri and her friends have perfect bodies anyone would want to proudly show off—not imperfect bodies they desperately want to hide behind oversized feathered suits.

The minute I realized my feathered *faux pas*, I fled into a corner of the large living room to await Kyle's return...and not thirty seconds later, someone grabbed my wing and shouted, "Hide, chicken! We're playing truth-or-dare hide-and-seek, and Mason Crenshaw is counting!"

I'd never heard of truth-or-dare hide-and-seek, of course. But that didn't stop me from running like a chicken with my head cut off to find a hiding spot. If Mason Crenshaw was playing the game, whatever it was, then I was playing it, too.

In short order, I had myself safely ensconced in a closet in a quiet back room. A minute after that, I'd taken my chicken head off to keep from hyperventilating. And a minute after *that*, the door to the closet swung open, and there he stood: *Mason Crenshaw*. Dressed like a pirate and looking gorgeous as ever in the moonlight streaming through a nearby window.

"You're a *chicken*?" Mason asked, a smirk lifting one side of his mouth.

Not knowing what else to say, I did what I always do in times of stress: I cracked a joke. "*Buh-gawk?*" I said feebly, flapping my arms...*and Mason laughed*. Okay, well, he kind of half-chuckled. But, *still*. It was an electrifying moment. I'd made the boy of my fantasies since fourth grade semi-chuckle *on purpose*.

Mason leaned against the open closet door. "Truth or dare, Savvy?"

Yet *another* electrifying moment. Prior to that moment, Mason had only addressed me as "Tutor Girl" during each and every one of our tutoring sessions in the library. Indeed, before then, I'd have bet anything Mason hadn't actually known my name.

I took a deep breath. "Truth," I said.

"Have you ever fantasized about having sex with me?" Mason asked, his dark eyes blazing.

My heart lurched into my throat. But since I'd agreed to tell the truth...I slowly nodded.

Mason bit his lip. "Are you a virgin, Savvy?"

"I've already answered a question."

"I get ten questions."

"*Ten?*"

"It's the rules of the game."

I opened and closed my mouth. Surely, if I'd known I'd have to answer ten questions, I'd have picked dare.

Mason smirked wickedly. "I'm guessing you're a virgin. Am I right?"

I nodded. "I've never even been kissed."

Mason leaned farther into the closet. "Do you wish you could kiss *me*?"

Holy shit. I nodded again.

"Right now?"

I nodded a third time.

Without hesitation, Mason entered the closet, shut the door behind him, placed his warm hands on my cheeks, and graced me with my first ever kiss. *And it was everything.* It was so amazing, in fact, I continued nodding each and every time Mason asked me another question until, eventually, my chicken suit was unzipped, my panties were down, and Mason's condom-covered erection was positioned at my entrance. I felt a quick flash of pain as Mason entered me. A couple thrusts. And then a faint rippling sensation inside me. And that was that. I was no longer a virgin.

I felt the urge to blurt "That's *it*?" But before I'd said a word, Mason pulled off his condom, put his index finger to his lips, and left the closet, leaving me sitting alone on top of my rumpled costume in the dark, feeling more like a deer in headlights than a chicken.

And now, here I am, two days later, walking down the

hallway of my high school. Mason's back is to me. He's laughing with a group of friends. And my heart is pounding.

When I reach Mason, I walk around to face him. "Hi," I say, shooting him a clipped wave. "I just wanted to tell you I had a nice time on Sa—"

Without warning, Mason grabs my arm and pulls me away from his friends.

"Let's not talk about what happened on Saturday night," he says when we're alone. "It's our little secret."

I'm flabbergasted. Isn't that my line? Whenever I've seen this scenario played out in teen movies, isn't it the *boy* who wants to brag about getting laid and the *girl* who wants to keep mum? "Why?" I ask lamely.

"It's the first rule of truth-or-dare hide-and-seek. Whatever happens in the hiding place stays in the hiding place."

Boom. Full understanding crashes down on me. "You're *ashamed* you slept with me?" I blurt.

"Sh," Mason says, looking around nervously. "Jesus, Savvy. No, I'm not *ashamed*. It's just that we don't fit together. You must know that."

I'm too embarrassed to reply. I'm well aware that Mason and I don't travel in the same social circles. But, honestly, I don't see how that means we don't *fit*. To the contrary, I think if we got together, we'd make an adorable "opposites attract" kind of couple.

Mason continues. "Look, I was willing to make your fantasies come true on Saturday night. But that's all it was: *wish fulfillment.* Be grateful for the awesome memory, and let's

11

just leave it at that." With that, Mason jogs down the hallway, leaving me standing alone, feeling dirty and stupid and ugly and fat and swearing to myself I'll never again give my body away to another asshole who doesn't love and respect and *appreciate* me as long as I fucking live.

CHAPTER ONE

SAVANNAH

Present Day
San Bernardino County, California

Wednesday, 12:08 p.m.
My legs and heart pumping and my mind reeling, I continue hiking up the steep mountain trail. I can't believe I lost my job this morning—and with zero notice or severance! And only two months after using every dime of my savings for the down payment on a fixer-upper condo in West LA!

Crap.

When I bought my condo, I knew a huge conglomerate was sniffing around my employer. But my boss assured me all employees of my company's cybersecurity division, especially an "up-and-coming hot shot" like me, would survive any rumored acquisition. "You've already made a name for yourself around here, Savvy," my boss said. "You're one of four people being considered for promotion to team manager. Trust me, if there's a merger, you'll be safe. *I guarantee it.*"

Of course, I relied on my boss's assurances and went ahead with the condo purchase. Why wouldn't I? I truly believed buying, renovating, and then flipping a condo for a tidy profit would be a fantastically *smart* thing for me—a twenty-three-year-old with her first corporate gig—to do. And now, here I am, eight weeks later, house-poor, shitcanned, and freaking the fuck out.

And yet...now that I think about it...the thing that's freaking me out the most in this moment isn't my finances. It's that I feel like I've been abruptly stripped of my *dream*. I wanted to become the youngest person to get promoted to team manager at Kidwell, Kasner & Barnes. I wanted it so badly, I could taste it. And I wasn't just sitting around wishing and hoping to make my dreams a reality. I was working my ass off. For the past month—on my *own* time during evenings and weekends while working on my personal laptop at home—I was slaving away on a secret project designed to get the attention of the decision-makers for the promotion. And now they'll never see my hard work!

My phone rings, and I stop on the dusty trail to check the screen. It's Kyle, my lifelong best friend. Surely, he's calling back after hearing the blubbering, pathetic voicemail I left him this morning.

"Hey," I say into my phone.

"They fired you with *no* notice?" Kyle bellows.

"None. And no severance, either. And this after my boss *guaranteed* my job would be safe." I sigh. "Why does every man in my life, other than you and Derek, lie to me? What am I doing wrong, Kyle?"

"You're not doing anything wrong. Getting laid off wasn't your fault. And neither was that whole clusterfuck with your dad."

At Kyle's mention of my father, I glance down at the ruby heart ring on my finger—the "valentine" my father gave me, his favorite Valentine, on my sixteenth birthday. I sigh audibly, my heart squeezing.

"Aw, Savage," Kyle says. "Are you okay?"

"I've been a whole lot better," I mutter. I glance around at the boulders and foliage surrounding me on the dusty trail. "But don't worry. Just being out here in nature and finally getting to hear a friendly voice today is working wonders. Derek is at a fitness conference in San Diego today and didn't pick up when I called."

"Back up. Did you just say you're in *nature*?"

"Yeah, I'm hiking up a mountain about two hours east of LA. It's this place Derek took me a couple weeks ago. We hiked to an overlook at the top, and Derek pulled out a bottle of champagne and two plastic cups and told me he'd developed feelings for me."

I smile at the amazing memory. Who knew the hot-as-hell personal trainer I hired eight months ago to whip me into shape for my upcoming five-year high school reunion would eventually become my hot-as-hell boyfriend?

"*Feelings?*" Kyle says.

I can't help smiling into the phone. "He told me he loves me."

"Wow, Savvy. Champagne and an 'I love you' at the top of a mountain? It doesn't get better than that."

Well, actually, it *does* get better than that, but I'm not a girl who has sex and tells, not even to Kyle. But the truth is that, after Derek shocked me by saying he loves me two weeks ago, he led me into a nearby thicket of trees, laid out a plaid blanket atop the pine needles and sticker balls littering the ground, stripped off my clothes, and made love to me in the dappled sunshine.

Kyle says, "So why'd you drive all the way out there to hike?"

"I wanted to show myself, in a tangible way, I'm strong and powerful and nothing, not even losing my dream job, can keep me down. A year ago, I couldn't have made it a quarter of the way up this steep trail, let alone all the way to the top. Plus, I figured if Derek can't be here to comfort me in person, then hiking to our special spot is the next best thing. But enough about me. What are *you* up to this fine Wednesday afternoon?"

"I'm in Denver, babysitting a rock star. Lucas Ford had a meltdown at his concert here last night, so I put him up in a hotel, and now I'm making sure he stays put and writes some songs like a good little rock star."

"Wow, Lucas Ford has been on a downward spiral lately, hasn't he? I thought I saw something about his leaked sex tape the other day."

"You sure did. Mr. Ford is the gift that keeps on giving." Kyle sighs with exasperation. "How the hell did I become a glorified babysitter for a living? I took a job with a record label because I wanted to discover awesome new artists, not fetch coffee and weed and babysit entitled rock stars."

"Aw, Kyle, I'm sorry. I know how excited you were to get that job."

"Meh. It's okay. The good news is I'm almost positive I'll still be able to make the reunion on Saturday night to see you."

"Actually, now that I'm unemployed, I'm not sure I'll be going to the reunion anymore."

"What? You have to go, Savvy."

"I'll still go to Vegas. My room at the Bellagio is prepaid for three nights, beginning tomorrow, and, of course, I want to see you. I'll probably hang out by the pool and go to the spa and stuff like that, so text me when you get there on Saturday, and we'll meet for drinks or whatever."

"No way. You're going to the reunion."

"Why? I wanted to go to show Mason Crenshaw and everyone else that the captain of the math and coding teams grew up to achieve the holy trinity of hotness: hot body, hot boyfriend, and hot career. What's the point in going *now* that I've only got two out of three?"

"Hey, two out of three ain't too shabby. Especially when, for eight freaking months, you've been consuming nothing but kale and boiled chicken and working out like a fiend for the sole purpose of making Mason Crenshaw's eyes bug out of his head at the reunion."

"I didn't get in shape for *Mason*. He was the dangling carrot I've used on myself to stay motivated during tough workouts. At the end of the day, I got fit and healthy to become my best self."

"Okay, Oprah. Regardless, you've got to come to the reunion for *me*. You need to be my hype-man and tell everyone I'm an actual music scout, not a glorified babysitter."

I sigh with resignation. "Fine. I'll go. But only because you said the magic word."

"Hype-man?"

"Oprah."

Kyle laughs. "Thanks, Savage. I can't wait to see you. And you've got to admit it'll be fun to have Mr. Fitness Trainer Man Candy on your arm in front of Mason Crenshaw."

I smile to myself at the thought. "True. That definitely won't suck. Well, thanks for cheering me up. I'm going to continue hiking up this lonely mountain now."

"Atta girl, Savage."

We say our goodbyes.

I continue hiking up the trail, and forty minutes later, I reach my destination: the overlook where Derek declared his love for me, right before leading me into the nearby thicket of trees.

Carefully, I creep to the edge of the steep drop-off and take in the sweeping views of the valley below...and, I'll be damned, as I take in the scenery before me, a deep-seated serenity washes over me. Yes, I lost my job today. And yes, six months ago, I found out my dad had a secret family—a longtime mistress with two young kids who apparently love him. But those setbacks don't define me. What defines me is that I respond to bad news by hiking to the top of a freaking mountain.

Suddenly, I want nothing more than to talk to Derek. Oh, man, he's going to flip his lid when he finds out his computer-nerd girlfriend hiked all the way to our special spot all by herself. With pride and excitement surging inside me, I pull out my phone and push the button to place the call...and the instant I hear the line ringing in my ear...I also hear a faraway ringing sound behind me, coming from the direction of the nearby thicket.

I whirl around. The distant ringing is coming from behind the thicket where Derek led me two weeks ago...and it's happening in perfect lockstep with the ringing in my ear.

Derek's outgoing voicemail message starts in my ear... at the precise instant the faraway ringing sound behind the trees...*stops.*

What the...?

Without leaving a message for Derek, I disconnect my call. And then, my heart pounding, I walk slowly toward the trees.

I enter the thicket. Pine needles and sticker balls begin crunching beneath my hiking boots. As if in a trance, I pass a large pine tree. And then another. Apparently, my feet know exactly where to go. I turn a corner and weave through some trees...

And there he is. *Derek.* Naked and having sex with a woman on top of the same plaid blanket he laid out for us two weeks ago on this very spot.

I stand frozen, my eyes taking in the horrific scene. Derek's muscular ass clenching and unclenching with each enthusiastic thrust. The two small piles of clothes and hiking boots perched on the edge of the blanket. The opened bottle of champagne and two plastic cups.

My gaze drifts to the naked woman writhing underneath Derek. She isn't particularly fit, I notice—and I'm quite certain I'm not making that observation out of spite or to body-shame the woman. God knows, even after eight months of rigorous diet and exercise, I'm no hard body myself. No, I'm certain my brain is making note of this woman's apparent fitness level and body shape as part of its rapid-fire deductive reasoning process. *That woman looks similar to the way I did when I first hired Derek eight months ago. Ergo, it seems reasonable to conclude she's also Derek's...*

Bile rises sharply in my throat. "Liar!" I scream, sending Derek and his new client scrambling off the blanket like cockroaches after a light has been flipped on. Shrieking, I gather up the woman's clothes and shoes off the blanket and toss them toward a nearby bush. *God speed, my gullible sister.* And then, I dump Derek's cell phone, clothes, and shoes onto the center of the blanket, add the opened bottle of champagne and two plastic cups onto the pile, fold the blanket over the top, and sprint at full speed with my booty in the direction of the overlook.

"Wait, Savvy!" Derek screams behind me.

But I'm not waiting. And Derek can't catch me, either. Not when he's barefoot and there's an infinite sea of prickle-balls and pine needles on the ground. Not when I'm a woman possessed and he's a naked guy trying to run after me with a hard-on and blue balls.

Panting, I reach the overlook. I stop on a dime, wind up like an Olympic shot putter, and hurl my entire blanketed treasure trove over the cliff.

"Noooo!" Derek calls out from a distance behind me.

I turn around, my eyes wild. "Enjoy your naked hike down the mountain, you lying, cheating sack of shit *con artist*!"

With that, I begin marching back down the dusty trail, muttering expletives to myself as I go. But just before I've turned a corner and disappeared from Derek's sightline for good, I throw up both middle fingers over my head in a final "fuck you" to the man—the *liar*—who told me he loved me solely to get into my pants. But my bravado is an act—a display of strength I don't actually feel. Indeed, the moment I turn a corner and I'm certain Derek can't see me, I lower my arms and hang my head...and melt into a sobbing mess.

CHAPTER TWO

SAVANNAH

"Another one, Cal," I say, holding up my empty glass to the bartender. He's a stout guy with a salt-and-pepper beard and black pleather vest, and he's my only friend in the world besides Kyle. "Let's keep that whisky coming."

When I got off the mountain about an hour ago, I tumbled into my SUV, my vision blurred by rage and rejection and humiliation, and drove east like a bat out of hell along the two-lane highway. I didn't know where I was headed or what misadventure I was hoping to find when I got there. But I knew I was about halfway between LA and Vegas and that there was nothing good waiting for me from whence I'd come. I didn't necessarily want to make it all the way to Vegas *today*. My prepaid three nights at the Bellagio start tomorrow night. But I knew I wanted to get as far away as possible from my money pit of a condo, my cheating ex-boyfriend, and my heartless ex-employer. Oh, and I also knew that after eight months of drinking nothing but lemon water in the name of "becoming my best self"—ha!—I now wanted booze. *And lots of it.*

After thirty minutes of driving, I came upon a small cluster of businesses along a straight stretch of highway. It was a cluster that included this shabby-looking bar, a gas station with an attached service garage, a motel, and a Mexican food joint. And, instantly, I knew I'd found my new home. I filled my gas tank, checked in to the rundown motel, stowed my laptop under my saggy bed, took a hot shower with the world's tiniest bar of soap, changed into jeans and a T-shirt, and trudged over to the Mexican place where I promptly scarfed down the burrito with the highest calorie count on the menu. After all that, I marched into this bar, put a dollar into the jukebox, and started pouring whiskey down my booze-hole.

And now, here I am, drinking, talking to the bartender, and listening to my song of choice on the jukebox: "Shattered Hearts" by none other than Kyle's favorite entitled rock star, Lucas Ford. When the song ends, I raise my glass to the jukebox. "To Lucas Ford and me!" I bellow. "And anyone else with a shattered heart!" With great flourish, I take a long guzzle of my whiskey drink and glance around the bar. "Hey, Cal!" I say to the bartender. I point to a framed headshot on the wall above the jukebox. "Who's that mustachioed Ken doll?"

Cal laughs. "Tom Selleck. He came in here to use the bathroom on his way to Vegas in 1993. And then he sat down on that stool right there and ordered a Diet Coke."

"Tom...?"

"*Selleck*."

I stare blankly.

"*Magnum P.I.?*" the bartender says. And then he hums what I assume is a theme song. "You know, the TV detective who drives around Hawaii in a red Ferrari?"

I shrug. "Doesn't ring a bell."

"It was a huge hit."

"In the nineties?" I ask.

"The eighties. How old are you?"

"Twenty-three." I point at him. "But don't underestimate me based on my tender age. I'm an up-and-coming 'hot shot,' Cal. One of four being considered for promotion to team manager." I snort and raise my drink to my lips and take a long gulp. "Seriously, Cal, I'm the motherfucking shit."

The bartender chuckles.

I'm about to say more to Cal—something witty and snarky and fabulous—when a beam of sunlight shoots across the bartender's face, signaling the opening of the front door behind me. Reflexively, I turn around to see what form of human has dared let the sunshine into my crypt...and my heart physically stops. *Whoa.* Forget that mustachioed TV detective on the wall. *This* guy is the hunk I'd want to take back to my motel room tonight if given half the chance.

The sexy dude entering the bar looks to be in his mid-twenties. He's holding a motorcycle helmet in one hand and a dark backpack in the other. He's got sandy hair, a chiseled jaw, and light eyes framed by bold eyebrows. His extremely fit body is clothed in a dark leather jacket, worn jeans, and a blue T-shirt that matches his stunning eyes. In short, he's perfect.

My heart thumping, I turn back around and take a long gulp of my drink and, a few seconds later, Mr. Perfect bellies up to the bar to my right.

The air between us fills with the delicious scents of him: leather, faint aftershave, and the great outdoors. He places his helmet atop the bar and his backpack on the ground and greets the bartender in a low, masculine voice. "Hey, man."

"What'll it be?" Cal replies, placing a cocktail napkin in front of the guy.

"Whatever will get me shitfaced and stupid in short order," comes Mr. Perfect's perfect reply.

"Great minds think alike," I murmur.

"Huh?"

I clear my throat. Under normal circumstances, I wouldn't initiate contact with a stranger in a bar, especially not a stranger who looks like this guy. But, today, normal rules don't apply, apparently. Today, I'm all out of fucks to give. "I said, 'Great minds think alike.' Meaning my plan is to get shitfaced and stupid in short order, too." I raise my drink. "Indeed, I'm well on my way. This is my second drink, and I'm a lightweight, especially after eight months of not drinking."

"Well, damn. As long as we're both getting shitfaced and stupid tonight, we should probably do it together, don't you think? Drinking is a lot like sex. You can do it alone, but it's a whole lot more fun with a partner."

I can't help returning his wicked smile. I motion to the stool next to me. "Please."

"Thanks." He settles himself and the delicious scents attached to him intensify. "So what are you drinking?" he asks.

"Whiskey sours," I say. "But, actually, I'm imbibing, not drinking. Because drinking is sad." I make a sad face. "But imbibing is *fun*." I make a happy face that makes him chuckle. "Actually, no, that was a lie," I say. "I'm not imbibing. I'm most definitely drinking. Drowning my sorrows, in fact. I've had a horribly shitty day, and I'm numbing the pain."

"Sorry to hear that. Is the whiskey doing the trick?"

I slap my face. "So far, so good."

"Perfect." He motions to Cal. "I'll have whatever the fuck this gorgeous woman is having. And add her drinks to my tab. A woman this beautiful, especially one having a horribly shitty day, can't pay for her own drinks. Not on my watch, anyway."

Every cell in my body spazzes out, all at once. "Thank you," I say, my cheeks blooming. "I appreciate it."

"My pleasure." He leans toward me. "I'm not doing it simply to be nice. I'm trying to seduce you after having a horribly shitty day myself."

"*Oh*. Wow. Thanks for letting me know."

He winks. "Sure thing."

The bartender slides a drink in front of Mr. Perfect, and he raises it to me. "Cheers," he says. "To getting shitfaced and stupid and numbing the pain."

"Cheers to that." I clink his glass. "Although I hope you're not planning to get *too* shitfaced and stupid. I'm quite certain Uber doesn't pick up out here in 1982, and I'd hate to see that thing turn into a brain bucket on you." I motion to his helmet on the bar.

"Thanks for your concern, but I won't be driving anywhere tonight, unfortunately. Hence, my horribly shitty day. My bike crapped out on me a couple miles back, and I had to push it until I came upon the garage across the street. As it turns out, they had to order a part, which means I'm stranded for at least a couple days."

I grimace sympathetically.

"And that was just the tip of the iceberg of my horribly

shitty day," he adds. He exhales. "So I've decided to get shitfaced and stupid, crash at the motel tonight, and figure out my game plan tomorrow morning."

"Great minds think alike again," I say. "That's my exact itinerary, as well. I've already booked my room at the motel."

"You're one step ahead of me there. I came straight to this bar after the garage. But don't worry about me. I promise I'll be crashing at the motel tonight." He flashes me a wicked smile and winks. "One way or another."

Holy crap. Did this sexy man just call his shot? Did he just imply he'll be sleeping with me in *my* room tonight? By George, I think he did. "So where were you headed when your bike broke down?" I ask.

"Vegas. What about you? Unless, of course, this place was your final destination."

"No, I stumbled upon this place by chance. I'm actually headed to Vegas, too. I grew up there, and my five-year high school reunion is this Saturday night."

I wait. Surely, he's going to try to bum a ride to Vegas from me now. And what will I say? It'd be no inconvenience for me to take him. And I'd thoroughly enjoy glancing over at him for three solid hours during the drive. And yet, on the other hand, I think I've seen this particular after-school special... and it didn't end well for the female driver who picked up a handsome stranger.

But, nope. Much to my surprise, he doesn't broach the subject. Instead, he takes a long sip of his drink and mutters, "If that's your second drink, then I've got some catching up to do."

I return his smirk. "If you want to keep up with me, then you'd better make your next drink a double." I throw back the rest of my drink and place my empty onto the bar next to his. "I'm not fucking around today. I'm done fucking around."

His eyes blaze. "Damn." He chuckles. "I hope you don't mind me saying this, but that was sexy as fuck."

I grin. "I don't mind you saying it at all."

"Good. Because it was." He motions to the bartender. "Hey, Cal. Another round. And on the recommendation of this sexy-as-fuck woman, you'd better make mine a double."

I can't breathe. My heart is medically palpitating. This is the most electrifying interaction with a man I've ever had in my life. I lean into his broad shoulder. "I hope you don't mind me saying this, but I think you're sexy as fuck, too."

"I don't mind you saying that at all. In fact, I'm thrilled to know the attraction is mutual." He sticks out his hand. "I'm Aiden, by the way. Nice to meet you."

I take his hand, and electricity zings and zaps across my flesh at the point of contact. "Savvy," I say. "But don't let the name fool you."

Aiden cocks his head to the side. "So does that mean your name is Savvy, but you're not *savvy*?"

I giggle. "Correct. My full name is Savannah. Savannah Valentine. But I've always been called Savvy. And that's just a ridiculous nickname for me because I'm the least savvy person you'll ever meet. I've got book smarts for days. But street smarts? Not so much."

"Sounds like we're a perfect match. I've got *street* smarts for days, but book smarts? Not so much."

"Wow. I'd totally pick you for my zombie apocalypse team, Aiden."

"I'm honored. Thanks. And I'd pick you."

"Thank you."

Aiden chuckles and leans his forearms on the bar. "So, tell me, Savvy Who Isn't Savvy, why's a smart, funny, pretty girl like you sitting in a bar in the middle of nowhere on a Wednesday afternoon, drowning your sorrows?"

Surprised, I look down at my ruby ring, my cheeks flushing.

Aiden adds quickly, "Unless, of course, you don't feel comfortable talking about it."

I look up. Aiden's eyes are warm and comforting and gorgeously blue. He's truly magnificent to behold. "No, I...I actually *want* to babble about what happened today. You just surprised me, that's all. The way you looked so genuinely interested and...compassionate."

He smiles and my heart flutters.

"Do you want the short or long version of my story?"

"Long, of course. I've got nowhere to go, remember? Tell me everything."

To emphasize his point, apparently, Aiden takes off his leather jacket and lays it carefully onto a stool, thereby treating me to the glorious sight of his muscled, tattooed arms peeking out of his tight T-shirt. His right forearm is inked with the frets of a guitar. Piano keys grace his left. Musical notes dance around his right bicep while two sets of numbers— specific dates, apparently—are inscribed on his left. *Damn.* He's gorgeous.

I take a deep breath and smile. "Okay. Um. The long version, it is..." I clear my throat. "Well, when I arrived at work this morning, I found out my employer had been acquired by a conglomerate, and my entire department was no more. No notice or severance given to any of us. See ya, wouldn't wanna be ya. We were unemployed."

"Brutal. Where'd you work?"

I put my hand on my heart like I'm saying the pledge of allegiance. "Kidwell, Kasner & Barnes. My dream job."

"Is that a law firm?"

"It's nothing now, thanks to the merger. But it *was* a full-service accounting and finance firm with a bunch of different divisions—accounting, finance, legal, cybersecurity."

"And that was your *dream* job?"

I blush. "Yes."

"Huh. Well, I'm really sorry you lost it, then."

"But that was only the first of the one-two punch of my day. Right after I found out I'd been shitcanned without notice or severance, I raced home, packed a bag, and drove to a mountain hike about forty-five minutes that way." I point. "And that's where I climbed to an overlook—the same overlook where my fitness trainer of the past eight months, this guy Derek who later became my boyfriend, took me to confess he'd fallen in love with me two weeks ago." I snort. "Can you guess what I discovered today at the top of that mountain?"

Aiden shrugs. "Derek screwing another woman?"

I'm flabbergasted. "How the hell did you know that?"

"It just seemed like the logical ending to this story."

"Man, you *do* have street smarts, don't you?" I shake my

head. "I didn't see that one coming *at all*."

"Sorry. He took you to a mountain to say 'I love you'? Sounds like a douche."

I laugh. "And you want to know the worst part of it? Derek didn't just *cheat* on me with that woman today. Clearly, he shamelessly *played* me like a freakin' fiddle, right from the start. About a month ago, I told Derek the pathetic, embarrassing story of how I got humiliated in high school by the captain of the football team and that I haven't had casual sex ever since. Not even once. So, obviously, he decided to say whatever he had to say to get into my pants."

I look at Aiden, expecting him to be smiling with me. But he's not. On the contrary, Aiden looks...highly disappointed. And, suddenly, it occurs to me I just told him I haven't had casual sex since high school. *Oh, my God.* Why did I say that? Clearly, the logical implication of that statement is that I'm not open to having casual sex with him tonight! And that's simply not true! Yes, the *old* Savvy Valentine swore off casual sex, thanks to Mason Crenshaw, but the new Savvy Valentine, the woman born today on top of that mountain, is a crazy, reckless, unpredictable woman with no more fucks to give! No. Actually, she's a woman with only *casual* fucks to give! "Hey, can I clarify something?" I blurt, my cheeks blazing. "I've got no prohibition against casual sex. The old me *used* to have sex only in committed relationships. That's why I said that to Derek. But now, after today, I'm thinking I'd much rather have casual sex with a guy who's up front with me than get sweet-talked by a liar who only wants to get laid."

Aiden brings his drink to his lips, but he can't hide his

amused smile. "Okay. Thanks for the clarification."

Oh, man. He's sexy. "Just thought you should know that."

"Duly noted." He winks. "So how old are you, Savvy? Twenty-three?"

"How'd you know?"

"You said you're headed to your five-year high school reunion." He taps his temple. "Street smarts."

"Damn. I guess those suckers can really come in handy, huh?"

We both chuckle.

"How old are you?" I ask.

"Twenty-four."

"Did you go to your five-year high school reunion last year? Got any tips for me?"

"I didn't have a reunion," Aiden says. "Because I didn't graduate. I dropped out of high school at sixteen. Got my GED a few years later. I'm dyslexic and didn't realize it until I was nineteen. Up until then, I thought I was just an idiot."

"Oh, my gosh. How horrible that it took so long for you to get diagnosed."

He shrugs. "High school wasn't my bag, anyway."

I'm genuinely surprised by that statement. Aiden looks like the kind of golden god who'd be voted prom king at any high school across America. Not to mention his stunning physique suggests he was a star athlete in every sport.

Aiden levels me with his ocean-blue eyes. "So what happened that one time you had casual sex with the captain of the football team in high school? Something tells me it's a good story."

"Well, I don't know if it's a *good* story. It's certainly an *embarrassing* story, like I said."

"Embarrassing stories are the best stories. Especially when they involve sex."

"Yeah, but this one is, like, DEFCON-one level embarrassing. The story begins with me in a chicken costume and gets worse for me from there."

He chuckles. "Well, shit, now you've got to tell me the story. I *love* chickens."

I roll my eyes.

"It's true. I had a little chicken coop in my backyard when I was growing up."

"Seriously?"

"Yup."

"How many chickens did you have?"

"A dozen or so at any given time." He grins. "I ate *a lot* of eggs growing up."

"Ah. That explains all *that.*" I motion to his muscular body. "It's all that protein you had in your formative years."

He laughs.

"Where did you grow up?" I ask.

"Tennessee. Just outside Nashville. I moved to California at fourteen."

"I thought I heard a little country boy in there."

"Yeah, my Tennessee tends to seep out a bit when I drink. Sorry, *imbibe.* When I'm stone-cold sober, I pass for a California native."

"Why on earth would you want to pass for a California boy? I think that little bit of Tennessee in your voice is sexy as hell."

Aiden levels me with a blue gaze that lights my panties on fire. "You think?"

My clit throbs like a jackhammer. "I do. I really, really do."

He laughs. "Good. Thank God this crazy attraction I'm feeling is mutual."

Oh, man. That's it. My lady boner is at full mast. If this boy were to ask me to "get out of here" and head to the motel down the road right now, I'd say fuck yes. In fact, I'm tempted to invite him to my room right now...

Aiden leans forward, his blue eyes trained on mine. "Tell me your embarrassing story, chicken girl," he whispers. "And, please, don't leave out a single embarrassing detail."

Every cell in my body is wigging out. Every hair on my head. My nipples are hard. My crotch is pulsing. *I want to have sex with this man.* I take a deep, steadying breath and clear my throat. "Okay, I'll tell you."

"Thank you."

"But only because you've said you've got a soft spot for chickens."

He chuckles. "I do. Hand to my heart, I do."

I open my mouth to begin my story, but Aiden raises his palm.

"Sorry. Hang on. How 'bout you tell me your story over tacos and beer down the road? My stomach's growling like a grizzly bear, and I want to make sure I give you my undivided attention."

"Great idea. I don't know how it's possible after the burrito I had earlier, but I'm pretty hungry, too."

Aiden rises from his chair, gallantly puts out his hand, and pulls me up. "Let's do it," he says, smiling. "The night is young and beautiful and so are we, chicken girl. So let's go paint that taco stand red."

CHAPTER THREE

SAVANNAH

Beer, beer, and more beer. Chips and salsa. Guacamole. Tacos. Smoldering looks and heated glances and hard nipples and a throbbing crotch. That's what's been on the menu at the Mexican place for the past hour and a half. Oh, and me babbling about everything I've been dying to get off my chest all day long. No, actually, for the past six months, ever since I heard the shattering news about my father and his secret family.

To start with, I told Aiden the story of how I lost my virginity to Mason Crenshaw five years ago at that Halloween party—the whole *fowl* story, you might say. And Aiden's reaction was so beautifully sympathetic, so compassionate and nonjudgmental, I found myself actually *laughing* with him about the embarrassing fiasco. Indeed, I felt so comfortable baring my soul to Aiden about Mason Crenshaw, I then launched into telling him the entire story of my father, too.

"When the shit hit the fan about my dad's mistress," I say, "he left my mom and started living with her and her two kids. I heard he married her last month."

Aiden looks sympathetic. "You had no idea he was juggling

this whole other life?"

"None. And neither did my mom."

"How is your mom doing?"

"Pretty good, actually. She lives with her sister in Phoenix now. The craziest part is my dad isn't some kind of Casanova. If you met him, you'd never think he could pull off having a secret life for five years. He's the head of the math department at UNLV. A really well-respected mathematician. Growing up, I *idolized* him."

"What's your relationship like now?"

I reflexively touch the ruby ring on my finger. "Nonexistent. I told him if I want to talk to him, I know where to find him at UNLV."

"Are you planning to see him while you're staying in Vegas?"

"No. When I originally booked my room at the Bellagio for three nights, my plan was to hang out with my dad for a couple days before the reunion. But, obviously, I don't want to see him now."

Aiden looks pained. He pushes his empty taco plate to the side and places his tattooed forearms onto the table. "You've had a rough go of it with men, haven't you, chicken girl? Mason Crenshaw, your dad, and now Derek?"

I nod and stuff down the lump suddenly forming in my throat.

"Please, accept my sincerest of apologies on behalf of my gender. We're not all douchebags and liars."

"I know that. I've known some really wonderful men in my life. I've just had a string of bad luck lately."

Aiden assesses me for a long moment. "So what's your plan now when it comes to men? Are you gonna swear off them for good or what?"

"No, I'm a hopeless romantic, unfortunately. Probably due to my last name. But I will say one thing: from now on, I'm going to stay firmly inside my safety zone when it comes to men." My heart lurches into my mouth. "When I'm looking for an actual *boyfriend*, that is," I sputter. "Obviously, not when I'm possibly looking to have a one-night stand with a sexy stranger I met in a bar in the middle of nowhere."

A huge smile begins spreading across his face, but he lifts his beer bottle to his lips to hide it.

We're silent for a moment, both of us exchanging flirtatious looks.

"What did you mean you're going to 'stay inside your safety zone with men'?" he finally asks.

"From now on, I'm going to go back to dating the kinds of guys I dated in college. When I was at Stanford, I only dated guys who—"

"You went to Stanford?"

"Yes."

"Wow. Isn't that where the Facebook guy went to college? You weren't kidding about those book smarts."

"I think you're thinking of the Snapchat guy. He went to Stanford. The Facebook guy, Mark Zuckerberg, went to Harvard but dropped out."

"Oh. Okay. Well, either way, you're obviously not a dumbshit."

I laugh. "No, I'm not. When it comes to book smarts, as I

mentioned."

"And that's all our zombie apocalypse team needs you for, sweetheart. I've got the street smarts covered, trust me. We're good."

"Phew. So relieved. I'd sure hate to get eaten by a zombie."

Aiden chuckles. "I'm sorry I interrupted you. Continue. At Stanford, you only dated guys who..."

"Who perceived me as being *way*, *way*, *way* out of their league. Total nerds with zero game who felt like being with me was the equivalent of being with Kate Upton."

Aiden looks appalled. "You were attracted to guys like that?"

"What? You've got something against nerds? Because, news flash, I'm a nerd."

"I've got absolutely nothing against nerds, especially if you're one. What I've got something against is you—or *anyone*—settling for being with someone when you feel zero chemistry."

"I didn't say I felt *zero* chemistry with my college boyfriends."

"You felt chemistry with them?"

"No," I admit. "Not at all."

He scowls. "Then you shouldn't have been with them. No matter how 'safe' you think you want to be, if you're with someone who doesn't get your motor running like crazy, someone you consider a charity case, then your soul will eventually wither and die along with your sex drive."

"Charity? Who said anything about *charity*? My boyfriends in college were sweet and kind. They treated me well. Did I care one way or the other about having sex with them? No, to be honest. I didn't. But I knew they'd never, ever dump me and that was of paramount importance to me. I felt *safe*."

"*Safety* is your paramount goal when dealing with members of the opposite sex?"

"In a relationship? Absolutely. Knowing I won't get hurt is far more important to me than feeling some crazy physical attraction, any day of the week."

Aiden is aghast. "You're assuming the two things are mutually exclusive—feeling safe and having physical attraction."

I consider my answer for a moment and realize that, yes, I *do* consider the two concepts mutually exclusive. "That's been my experience, yes," I say. "Life is full of tradeoffs. That's one of them, and I'm perfectly fine with that. The safest boys make the best boyfriends."

Aiden looks absolutely floored. "Did you at least *become* physically attracted over time to the guys who—"

"No."

Aiden's mouth hangs open for a moment. "Jesus, Savvy," he mutters. He rubs his forehead. "Look, I know you've been fucked over by men. I get that. But you can't date guys simply because you're sure they won't *dump* you. You should be experiencing white-hot chemistry, every time. Find yourself a guy who makes you see God."

I shrug. "There are varying approaches to dating. This particular approach suits me and my needs. Case in point, I strayed from my safety zone with Derek the Douchebag, and look where that got me. He played me for a fool."

"Did he make you see God?"

I snort. "No. Not even close. But he was, you know, highly physically attractive, so I didn't view him as a safe bet. And, clearly, he wasn't one."

Aiden rolls his eyes. "Seriously, Savvy. This is pathetic, no offense. Why date anyone at all if your only goal is *not* getting dumped? That's like hiking up a mountain with the sole goal of *not* falling off a cliff. You should climb to feel *alive*. To reach the peak. Not to *not* fall off the edge."

"Okay, that's a horrible analogy. Having hiked up a mountain earlier today, I can confidently tell you that *not* falling off the edge was a hugely important part of the experience."

"Yeah, but *not* falling off isn't *why* you went on the hike in the first place, was it?"

I cross my arms over my chest. The boy's got a point. *Damn.*

"Okay, fuck it. Never mind. Bad analogy," Aiden says, clearly misunderstanding my silence. "All I know is I'd rather be alone with my guitar, my hand, and a bottle of lube than get with *anyone* who doesn't make me hard as a rock." His eyes darken with heat. "And that goes the same if we're talking about an actual relationship or a possible one-night stand with a sexy, funny, smart, hot mess of a girl I might happen to meet in a bar in the middle of nowhere."

I hold his heated gaze, my chest heaving. *Holy shit. I want him.*

Aiden leans forward and whispers, "You've never experienced white-hot chemistry, have you, Savvy?"

My heart is thumping in my ears. My clit is pounding. *I want him.* "I'm not sure."

"Then you haven't."

"Maybe, I have. I'm just not sure."

"There's no such thing as 'maybe' with this. If you'd experienced the kind of white-hot chemistry I'm talking about, you'd know it. Trust me, when you see God during sex, you never forget it."

I feel my cheeks blaze. My breathing feels labored. I open and close my mouth. *I want him.*

Aiden leans forward. "Derek the Douchebag *never* curled your toes? Not even after his fancy declaration of love at the top of that mountain?"

I shake my head. "No. Derek was a total dud. But it wasn't his fault. I was physically attracted to Derek, generally speaking, and flattered a guy with big ol' muscles and a dazzling smile was interested in pursuing a relationship with a girl like me—or so I *thought*. But what I was most excited about when it came to Derek, if I'm being honest, was the idea of getting to parade him around as my boyfriend at my high school reunion. Basically, I wanted to bring him to the reunion and let Mason Crenshaw see a guy kind of like *him* actually found me attractive." I roll my eyes. "Frankly, I think a piece of me knew all along Derek was lying to me, so I didn't fully...you know..." I shift in my seat. "*Relax* with him when it counted."

Aiden licks his lips, leans over the orange Formica table, and whispers. "Has *anyone* made you see God? *Ever?*"

My cheeks blaze. "Define that phrase, please."

He smiles wickedly. "Well, let's start with the basics. Has

any guy ever given you a simple orgasm?"

I shake my head. "Just me. When I'm alone."

He leans back. "Wow. That's a travesty, Savvy."

I shrug. "It's okay. Like I said, life is full of tradeoffs. With Derek, I didn't care so much about having good physical chemistry with him because I was so damned excited to get to bring him to my reunion and show him off."

He grimaces. "It means *that* much to you to bring a date to your reunion?"

"Well, *no*. Okay, yes."

Aiden exhales. "Shit." He pauses for a very long beat before muttering, "I wish I could be your date to that reunion, but—"

"Thank you!" I blurt. I shoot up from my chair, unable to contain my excitement. "I'd *love* to introduce you as my 'boyfriend' at the reunion."

Aiden looks stricken. "Oh, shit. No. You misunderstood me, Savvy. I was saying I *wish* I could go with you. And I *do*. But I honestly can't. I've got to be at this stupid birthday party on Saturday night in Vegas. Not for fun. For...work."

Mortified, I lower myself back onto my chair. "Oh. I shouldn't have... Sorry."

"Don't be sorry. I was being sincere. I'd love to go. Honestly, I'd cancel the job if I could, but the thing is my dad really needs money and—"

"No need to explain," I say. "I just misunderstood. It's fine."

"I'm sorry. If I could go, I'd—"

"No need to apologize. Thank you for even wanting

to go." I clear my throat and force a smile. "New topic. I've monopolized this entire conversation. Shame on me." I take a deep breath and widen my fake smile, my stomach churning. "Tell me about you. You said you moved to California at fourteen?"

Aiden looks tormented. "Shit. Savvy—"

"*Please*, Aiden. Don't give it another thought." Again, I force a smile. "Where in California do you live?"

Aiden rakes his hand through his sandy hair. "I live in LA," he says softly.

"Hey, so do I," I chirp. "I just bought a condo in West LA. Where do you live?"

"Silver Lake," he says softly.

"I love Silver Lake!" I say brightly. And then I babble lamely for an inordinately long time about how much I "adore" Silver Lake—a hipster area of LA across town from my condo.

After a bit, when it's clear I've run out of steam regarding all things Silver Lake, Aiden stands and indicates my empty bottle. "Another one?"

"Sure," I say, my chest tight. "Thanks."

And off Aiden goes to the front counter across the small restaurant, his body language stiff.

As I watch Aiden's gorgeous ass walking away from me, I scream at myself internally. *Take a chill pill, Savvy Valentine! First you begged the guy to come to your reunion and then you made it sound like you'll be stalking him when you get back to LA! Slow your roll, freak job! When he gets back to the table, make it clear you definitely want to have sex with him tonight and won't be stalking him afterward. Because that's how casual sex works, Savvy. Bang and goodbye. Bang and goodbye. Bang and freaking goodbye!*

Aiden appears at the edge of our table, holding two beer bottles. "Here you go. Nice and cold for ya."

"Thanks."

He slips back into his seat and raises his bottle to me. "Cheers to you, Savvy Who Isn't Savvy. My trusty partner in a zombie apocalypse."

"And to you, Aiden Who Isn't Ugly. I'm fifty percent confident we'd avoid getting eaten."

"I'll take those odds."

We clink. And drink. And then stare at each other awkwardly.

"So...tell me about your life in Tennessee," I say. "You said you moved to California at fourteen. What was your childhood like?"

He pauses, apparently considering his answer. "Well, let's see. I grew up outside of Nashville in a little house with a huge backyard. Like I said, we had a little chicken coop out back. A couple dogs. When I was really little, I lived with both my mother and grandfather. My mom was always in and out because of her job, but she loved me. I never doubted that, whether she was physically around or not."

"What was her job?"

"She was a professional backup singer for a whole bunch of different bands, so she was always heading out on one tour or another. Whenever she was gone, I stayed home with Gramps. Her father. And that was perfectly fine with me. I worshiped the ground he walked on." He looks wistful for a long beat.

"And then my mother died when I was eight, and it was just Gramps and me and our chickens and dogs. And then Gramps died of a heart attack right after I turned fourteen. And that's when I moved to California."

"Oh, Aiden. I'm so sorry." My eyes lock on the numbers inked on Aiden's bicep—and I instantly surmise they're the dates his mother and grandfather died. "How did your mother pass away?"

"A bus accident. She was on tour with a pretty popular country band, and their tour bus crashed. My mother and the band's lead singer both died. The crash was all over the news, but nobody cared about anybody but the leader singer. Mom was always referred to as 'and another member of the band.'"

"I'm so sorry."

"Thanks."

I'm quiet for a moment, trying to process the tragic losses Aiden has suffered. "Did you move to California to be with family or...?"

"Yeah. When Gramps died, I had a temporary guardian in Nashville at first, just to avoid being taken into foster care. But then she told me she really couldn't keep me more than a couple weeks at most, so I knew I'd have to get the hell out of there to avoid being taken into custody. So off I went in the middle of the night to LA. My mother had told my grandfather the name of my father and that he was from LA. And he'd told me, thank God."

I'm floored. "You went across the country all by yourself at age fourteen to find a father you'd never met before?"

Aiden shrugs. "I had nothing to lose."

"Oh, Aiden."

"I was used to being independent. My grandfather wasn't the kind of man who cut your meat for you."

I look at his face and suddenly realize there's a toughness there I didn't notice before. A steeliness. "And you found your father?"

"I sure did."

"How did he react when you showed up out of the blue on his doorstep? Was he shocked?"

He chuckles. "To put it mildly. He had no idea I existed. But he took me in that very day without hesitation and never looked back."

"Wow. Did he already have other kids? Was he married?"

Aiden shakes his head, grinning. "No. My dad isn't a 'married with children' kind of guy. He's a rolling stone, my dad. He was twenty-one when he got with my mother. It was a summer tour for a big country band. Mom was twenty-two and singing backup. Dad was part of the crew. Apparently, they had quite the passionate love affair that summer. But when the tour ended, so did their relationship. Dad immediately hopped on another tour. Mom went back home to Nashville to hang out with her dad for a bit and do some studio work. And that's when she found out she was pregnant."

"And she didn't tell him?"

"She didn't see the point. She told Gramps his name and age and stuff. The general story. But she said her future baby would be better off growing up without a father at all than one who didn't call on birthdays. And that was that. She didn't even put my father's name on my birth certificate."

"So did your father demand a paternity test when you showed up out of nowhere fourteen years later?"

"There was no need. I'm his spitting image. To see us together is like seeing the same man, only twenty years apart. My dad saw me on his doorstep, picked his jaw up off the ground, and took me in." Aiden chuckles. "Dad loves to say it was love at first sight when he saw me. But that's only because I look so damned much like *him*."

We both laugh.

And my heart flutters at the adorable look on his face.

"Seriously, though," Aiden says. "I'll be grateful to my father 'til the day I die for taking me in the way he did. He's not a saint by any stretch, my dad. In fact, he's a total fuck-up in some major ways." He rolls his eyes. "But if my father hadn't taken me in and loved me like he did, no questions asked, no conditions, no hesitations, then I would have been fourteen and living on the streets of LA, doing whatever fucked-up kind of hustle I had to do to survive. As far as I'm concerned, my dad literally saved my life, and I'll never, ever forget it."

I look down at the ring on my hand, thoughts of my own father making my heart squeeze. "I'm sorry you've had such a hard road in life," I say softly. "It breaks my heart to think about the losses you've endured, Aiden."

He brings his beer to his lips. "Meh. I'm a survivor. If you want to feel sorry for someone, feel sorry for my poor grandfather. When my mother died, that poor man died along with her. For the longest time, he didn't even want to go into the studio, that was how brokenhearted he was."

"The studio?"

"The recording studio. My gramps was a session musician."

"What's that?"

"Sorry. I forget laypeople don't know. If an artist doesn't have a band of their own, or maybe they don't have a particular instrument in their usual band, then they hire a session musician to play on their record. Session musicians aren't the guys who get the fame or fortune. But people in the music business *always* know the best ones—and everyone knew my gramps was the best of the best. He was a legend. The biggest names in the music industry always wanted my grandfather on their records. Over the decades, he wound up playing for just about every icon you can possibly think of—from country to rock to soul."

I glance at the music-themed tattoos on Aiden's arms. "Did you follow in your grandfather's footsteps?"

"I'm a musician, yeah. But I mostly play live, not in the studio. Unfortunately, I can't seem to make a living on music alone the way both my mother and grandfather did. I live for music, for sure. It's in my blood. But I've got to have a day job to survive, especially in a city as expensive as LA."

"What's your day job?"

"Construction. Handyman. Odd jobs. I live in an apartment complex and get half off my rent for fixing whatever might break. And then I pick up as many music gigs as I possibly can, no matter what the job. I just play and play and play. No job too small. I also do some busking."

I indicate the tattoos on his forearms. "You play guitar and piano?"

"Yeah, but guitar is my preferred instrument. That's what I'm known for. I sub on guitar for a bunch of different bands in LA."

"What do you mean, you 'sub' on guitar?"

"Are you sure I'm not boring you?" he asks. "I feel like I'm talking way too much."

"Not at all. I'm utterly fascinated," I assure him. And I'm telling the God's truth. Indeed, I'm not merely fascinated, I'm enchanted. Enthralled. Utterly and completely spellbound.

"I never talk about myself like this," Aiden mumbles. "How are you getting me to talk like this? Have you cast some kind of spell on me?"

My heart leaps. Could Aiden possibly be feeling as drawn to me as I am to him? I put my elbow on the table and my chin in my palm and gaze at him with what must be little hearts for eyes. "I'm just listening with rapt attention, the same way you listened to me when I talked earlier. Now, come on. Don't clam up on me now, Aiden Who Isn't Ugly. You were telling me about how you sub on guitar."

Aiden drags his teeth over his lower lip for a brief moment, making my clit pulse and throb with desire. "Yeah, whenever a band's guitarist can't make a gig for whatever reason, they call me and I come running. I also do session work whenever I can get it. But that's rare. And I have a solo acoustic gig at this popular brunch place in Silver Lake on Sundays. It's nothing fancy—just me singing and playing my acoustic guitar. But they let me play whatever I want, even my originals, and the tips are incredible. It's by far my highest-paying music gig every week."

"Are you playing a solo gig at that birthday party on

Saturday night or is it with a band?"

Aiden's face turns visibly red. He looks down at the table. "It's a...solo gig."

Holy hell. Is Aiden *embarrassed* to be playing at a birthday party? Have they hired him to play cheesy eighties music or something like that, rather than his originals? Well, he shouldn't be embarrassed, no matter what he's been hired to play. Not everyone can be a legendary session musician like his grandfather or make their living playing songs they've written. I touch Aiden's hand across the table. "I think it's awesome you've been hired to play at a birthday party, no matter what you'll be playing. If I can't parade you around in front of Mason Crenshaw at my stupid reunion, then I'm elated it's because you'll be earning money making music—doing what you were born to do."

"How do you know I was born to make music? You haven't heard me play."

"The way your face lights up when you talk about making music, it's clear music is your calling."

Aiden's features soften. "Thanks for knowing that about me, Savvy."

"Well, I'm not exactly reading tea leaves here. You wear your passion for music on your sleeve." I motion to his tattoos. "*Literally*. I said I have no street smarts, Aiden. I didn't say I'm a moron."

We both laugh.

"God, you're so amazing, Savvy, you know that? I really do wish I could have gone to that reunion of yours. I would have dry humped you in front of Mason Crenshaw like nobody's business."

"It's okay. If you can't dry hump me in front of Mason Crenshaw, I'm thrilled it's because you've got a paying gig." I bite my lip, mustering my courage. I take a deep breath. "But, um, actually...would you mind doing me a favor? Would you take a quick selfie with me where you pretend to drool all over me? I'd love to whip out a photo of my 'hot boyfriend who's totally obsessed with me' at the reunion. Ideally, I'd whip it out when Mason happened to be walking past..."

Aiden hoots and pats his thigh. "Come on, chicken girl! Let's take a selfie that will make Mason Crenshaw feel like the asshole he is."

I spring up from my chair, squealing with excitement and thanking him profusely.

"Oh, and, just so you know," Aiden says. "I won't be *pretending* to drool all over you in the shot. When it comes to you, sexy girl, any and all drool will be the real thing."

CHAPTER FOUR

SAVANNAH

From my perch on Aiden's lap, I snap a selfie of him kissing my cheek. And I think our photo shoot is done. But then Aiden surprises me by skimming his lips down my neck after the photo. And then nipping and kissing my neck. I'm not sure if he's simply hamming it up for the camera, so I snap a few more shots as he kisses me. I run my free hand through his hair, shuddering with arousal as he begins working his way up my neck toward my jawline... And then I turn my head, ever so slightly, to greet his approaching mouth...and our lips meet.

For a brief moment, Aiden kisses me tentatively, like he's asking for permission. And when I give it to him, his tongue slides into my mouth and tangles with mine, and every nerve ending in my body zaps and zings with outrageous arousal. I feel his steely hard-on underneath me, and I grind myself into it. Kissing him voraciously now, I slide my arms around Aiden's neck and lose myself to the glorious pleasure of our hungry kiss. Holy hell, this is the best kiss of my life.

For several minutes, Aiden and I kiss and kiss like our lives depend on it, more and more passionately—our hunger and yearning boiling over to a breaking point—until, finally,

Aiden pulls away from me, his eyelids half-mast, his cheeks flushed, his hard-on driving into me. He whispers, "Did you get the shot?"

"*Oh*," I say, my cheeks flushing. "No, I...got distracted."

"You had one job, chicken girl," he says. He flashes me a cocky smile that tells me he's joking around. "*One job.*"

I bite my lower lip. "Well, damn. I'm sorry. I guess we'll just have to do it again."

"I guess so." He swipes his thumb across my lower lip, making my crotch throb. And then he leans in slowly and kisses me again. And this time, despite the heart-stopping pleasure I'm experiencing, I somehow manage to snap a few haphazard selfies of us, just for the sheer hell of it.

When Aiden and I pull away from each other's lips this time, I whisper, "I'm pretty sure I got the shot that time."

"Oh, yeah?" He chuckles. "Let me see."

I swipe into my photos, and we both gasp at the image on my screen.

"Jesus," Aiden whispers. "We look like we're about to burst into flames."

"Talk about white-hot chemistry," I say. "Holy hell, Aiden."

"Told you I like chickens."

"Can I send this shot to Derek? I want him to see I'm not sitting around crying into a pint of Ben & Jerry's tonight. That I left that mountain today and wound up macking down on a dude who's ten million times hotter than he is."

"Fuck yeah. Send it."

I snort. "Now, in a perfect world, I wouldn't be sending

Derek photos of me *kissing* you. I'd be sending him photos of me and you doing a whole lot more than that. But—"

"Let's do it," Aiden says. "I'm in."

My eyebrows ride up. I open and close my mouth. Did I just invite him to fuck me for some photos? By George, I think I did. "In my motel room?" I choke out.

Aiden smirks. "Was that an invitation, Savvy Who Isn't Savvy?"

I ponder my answer for a half second and realize the naked truth: I want him. On camera. Off camera. Honestly, the photo thing was nothing but a ruse to get this gorgeous, sexy man into my bed. "Yes," I say. "It was an invitation. You're cordially invited to stay with me in my motel room tonight, Aiden Who Isn't Ugly."

"Thank you," he says, his eyes blazing. He motions. "Let's go, baby."

I get up from the bulge in Aiden's lap and hold out my hand to him. "The night is young and gorgeous, and so are we," I say with a mischievous smile. "Let's go make a porno in my motel room."

CHAPTER FIVE

AIDEN

Wednesday, 10:12 p.m.

Man, she's an easy mark.

That's what I'm thinking as I walk with Savvy in the warm night air from the taco place to the motel while listening to her belt out "Irreplaceable" by Beyoncé at the top of her lungs.

Actually, no. Let me correct that thought: Man, Savvy *would* be an easy mark *if* I were still on the con—like I was with Dad back in the day. Which I'm *not* and haven't been ever since we got pinched and went to prison. Talk about a guy getting scared straight. But yeah, *if* I were still playing the game with Dad, then there's no doubt in my mind I'd be shaking my head right now and thinking holy shit, this adorable girl is the easiest mark of my illustrious career.

I mean, for God's sake, Savvy straight-up *told* me she's gullible. That's what "not being savvy" and "not having street smarts" mean, after all. And if I'd missed it the first time, Savvy then went on to regale me with story after story to convince me of her lack of savviness. Jesus Christ! It was all I could do not to take that beautiful, sweet, sexy girl into my arms and say, "Listen to me, sweetheart. You're lucky you're telling this stuff to *me*—because I happen to be a reformed grifter—a true Boy Scout these days. But the next time you start talking to a stranger you met in a bar in the middle of nowhere about how *not* savvy you are, you might not get quite so lucky."

As Savvy continues singing and walking, she grabs my arm and leans her cheek against my shoulder—and that simple, affectionate, *trusting* touch makes my heart squeeze. What kind of spell is this pretty, sexy girl casting on me? I've never felt such an immediate spark. Is it the whiskey? Because I definitely feel buzzed. Really buzzed. But I truly don't think it's from the alcohol.

Savvy finishes her song, and I whoop my approval.

"Thank you. Thank you very much," Savvy says, doing her best Elvis impression.

I laugh. "You're so Vegas."

"Hey, you can take the girl out of Vegas, but not the Vegas out of the girl." She giggles. "Would you like me to sing another one?"

"Hell yeah. Hit me with another *Hell Hath No Fury Like a Woman Scorned Song*, baby."

Savvy bites the tip of her finger, apparently mulling her options, and then begins belting out "You Oughta Know" by Alanis Morissette. And my heart skips a beat, yet again.

How is this possible? When I first laid eyes on Savvy sitting at the bar today, I didn't think, *Ah, there's the girl who's going to help me forget I'm in the worst shitstorm of my life.* On the contrary, when I saw Savvy sitting at that bar, I thought, *Now, there's the girl I'm gonna get to drive me to Vegas tomorrow.* That's all I thought. One look at her sitting there, looking like a sexy, hot mess, and I knew I could sweet-talk her into doing anything I wanted. Literally. And so, of course, I beelined right to her, sat myself down, and flirted my ass off. And that was *before* Savvy told me she was headed to Vegas herself! Once I found out *that* little nugget, I knew I wouldn't have to say a damned thing to Savvy about her driving me to my final destination—that she'd eventually offer to do it without prompting.

And then, somewhere along the line, I completely forgot about my intention to use Savvy for a ride. Indeed, even in the midst of my present panic, I just started...digging her. Like, big-time. And that's when I knew using her wasn't an option. She was off-limits to any kind of con, no matter how desperate I feel. And that was *before* we went to the taco place and she started telling me all the ways she's been fucked over by men in her life!

"Home sweet home," Savvy says, pulling me out of my thoughts—and I realize we're standing in front of the motel. "This way." Savvy indicates an outdoor hallway, and I follow her past a bunch of rooms. She comes to a stop in front of room 112 and holds up a keycard. "Are you ready to make a porno with me, Aiden Who Isn't Ugly?"

Oh, my God. *This girl.* I want her so fucking bad. But, shit, I'm suddenly hearing my parole officer's voice in my ear, telling me to never, ever risk fucking a drunk girl. "*You never know what regrets they might have in the morning, Aiden,*" my parole officer warned. "*And if she accuses you of something later, who will they believe? The girl or the felon?*"

"Hang on," I choke out as Savvy opens her door. "Are you

sure about this? You've been drinking. I want you to be sure."

Savvy snorts. "It's not the booze making me want to have sex with you. I've wanted to have sex with you since the minute I laid eyes on you. The booze is simply giving me courage to do what I want to do."

Okay, that addresses the first potential concern. But what about the second one? "You understand this is casual, right?" I say. "There's no possibility of a tomorrow for us. This is a one-night thing."

Savvy raises an eyebrow. "No possibility of a tomorrow?" She screws up her face. "But I was assuming I was going to drive you to Las Vegas tomorrow, since I'm headed there myself, anyway. You don't want me to take you?"

"Oh. Yeah. I'd really appreciate a ride. Thanks."

"Sure thing."

"I just want to be sure you understand I'm gonna say goodbye to you when we get there. My life is a shitstorm right now, Savvy. The timing isn't right for me to start something with anyone right now, even someone as amazing as you."

Savvy smiles broadly and waves off my concerns. "You're so sweet to make that perfectly clear for me. Thank you. But I'm good. I'm on the rebound, remember? The last thing I should be doing is chasing after some gorgeous guy I met in a bar in the middle of nowhere. Let's just make a porno tonight and drive to Vegas tomorrow, and that will be that. It'll be a great memory for both of us."

I sigh with relief. "Sounds good."

"So we're good?"

"We're good."

She smiles and holds up her keycard suggestively. And then she giggles and opens the door with flourish. "Now, please, for the love of God, get your hot ass into my motel room and let's make a porno."

CHAPTER SIX

AIDEN

Savvy turns around from closing the door, throws her arms around my neck, and giggles. "This is gonna be so *fun!*"

"Hang on, baby." I pull away from her voracious lips, though it pains me to do it. "We've got to set some ground rules for the porno to protect you."

"But I want to go crazy," she whispers, her dark eyes ablaze. "I want to be *bad.*"

My dick jolts, but I pull back from her lips again. "Listen to me, chicken girl. If Derek decides to post the videos as revenge porn, you need to be able to say it's not you. No faces in any of the videos, okay? *No faces.*"

"Gotcha. Everything will be shot from the neck down. That's common sense." She goes in for a kiss again but then jerks back. "Wait. How will Derek know it's me in the videos, having the time of my life with the hottest guy on the planet, if he can't see my face? I don't want him thinking I sent him some video clips I pulled off Pornhub. I want him to know for sure it's *me.*"

I mull that for a moment, and when inspiration strikes, I grab her hand and indicate the ruby ring on her finger. "Do you usually wear this ring?"

"Always. My dad gave it to me for my sweet sixteen. It's my most-prized possession."

"You think Derek will recognize it?"

She nods. "He asked me about it once, and I told him all about it."

"Okay, then. This ring is going to be the star of our porno, baby. Front and center in every video we make. Derek will know it's you, but the world won't."

Savvy squeals with glee.

"And one more thing," I say. "I can't believe I'm about to say this, but *don't* say my name, okay?" I laugh. "No names in the heat of passion, chicken girl."

"Yes, sir. No faces. No names. Ring front and center. Can we get started now with the bow chicka wow wow, please?"

Oh, my God. *This girl.* "Let's do it. With pleasure."

Savvy nuzzles my nose with hers, a huge grin on her pretty face. "You're a prince among men, Aiden."

My dick is rock hard. My heart is thudding in my chest. I'm not a prince. Not even close. But tonight, with Savvy in my arms, I sure feel like one. "And you're my sexy porno princess," I whisper, just before leaning in and kissing her.

She presses her body against mine and rubs herself against my hard-on. "Thank you," she whispers.

"Don't thank me," I say. "I don't get hard like this for charity."

I kiss her and she responds passionately. And that's it. We're both on fire. Kissing and groping and stripping off our clothes.

We tumble onto the bed in our underwear.

"I want you so much," I say. And it's the God's truth. Savvy's near-naked body is blowing my mind. She's got tits I could get lost in. Hips I can't wait to grip when I fuck her from behind. Hard, pink nipples that make my mouth water at the sight of them. Everything about Savvy's curvy body brings out a primal instinct in me to touch and lick and suck and fuck.

Savvy grabs her phone off the mattress next to us. "Ready to become a porn star?"

I grin. I have no idea what the hell kind of "porno" Savvy's planning to shoot tonight—if the video she's got in mind will be PG-13 or triple X. But I'm down for whatever it is. "Ready."

And off we go.

Savvy shoots a video of her ringed hand exploring the ridges of my abs and then sliding toward the waistband of my briefs, heading toward the hard bulge poking from behind the fabric.

I hold my breath with anticipation, aching to feel her fingers on my cock, but just before her hand breaches the waistband of my briefs, she looks up at me, her eyes clearly asking for permission.

"Do it," I whisper, a wicked grin on my face.

She blushes and nods...and captures video of her ringed hand peeling my briefs down and off...and then sliding back up my thighs and finally, blessedly, gripping my hard, aching cock. My tip is shiny with my need. Beaded with wetness. I open my mouth to say something reassuring, to tell Savvy we can go as slow as she wants, but before I get a word out, Savvy points her camera straight at my cock and captures video of her thumb swirling the wetness pooled on my tip.

I jolt with arousal. "Let the porno begin," I whisper.

And away we go.

First off, Savvy records her ringed hand giving me a hand job. And then we move on to recording my hard, straining cock fucking the canyon between her ample tits as the star of our porno—her ringed hand—gropes her nipples and breasts.

When I'm way too turned on to continue titty-fucking her, I guide Savvy onto her back on the mattress and whisper in her ear. "Time to make you come," I say softly. I peel the camera out of Savvy's hand and toss it onto the mattress. "I'm gonna make you feel so fucking good, baby." I slide my fingers between her legs. I'm met with warm wetness and a loud, sexy moan by Savvy that makes my cock jolt and my balls tighten. I start working her hard, swollen clit around and around. I kiss her breasts. Suck her nipples. Bite her neck and kiss her lips...all while working her hard clit rhythmically around and around. In short order, I've got Savvy moaning and writhing furiously against me. Her body is telling me I've got her right where I want her.

"Oh, God, Aiden," Savvy chokes out. "Get the camera. Oh, God, Aiden."

"No names," I remind her, grabbing the phone with my free hand.

Savvy digs her fingernails into my forearm. "Keep going just like that," she says. "*Oh, God.*"

"Put your hand on mine," I command. "Get the ring in the shot when you come."

Savvy does as she's told, even as she's writhing and

moaning and whimpering against me, and half a second later, she comes against my fingers with a long, low moan.

"That's it," I whisper. I throw the camera down and kiss her voraciously while sliding my wet fingers inside her and straight to her G-spot. My chest heaving and my dick seeping with arousal, I begin massaging that mysterious bundle of nerves, swiping my fingers across it with confident, firm strokes, until Savvy's bucking and gyrating and writhing at my touch like a woman possessed.

"Video!" she chokes out. "Get it on video!"

With my free hand, I grab her phone again and point it at my hand between her legs and she slides her ringed hand on top of mine just before her body stiffens sharply and then begins undulating against my hand.

"That's it, sexy girl," I growl as Savvy groans and moans and comes against me. I raise my voice for the benefit of the camera. "Hey, Douchebag! Are you having fun watching me get this sexy girl off the way you never could?"

Savvy's muscles stop warping and clenching against my fingers. She lets out a long, satisfied sigh, followed by a happy little moan. Clearly, her climax was a good one. "Hey, Douchebag," she purrs toward the camera. Her brow is sweaty. "Guess what? I just had the best orgasm of my life. Oh, and you want to know what else? I was faking it with you *all three times.*"

I burst out laughing and point the camera at my fingers, which are, at this moment, swirling gently over the insides of Savvy's creamy thighs. "Hey, Douchebag. Watch close now. I'm gonna make her come again. But this time, through her

A-spot. Oh, you've never even heard of that spot? Yeah, no shit, you haven't, D-bag. Watch and learn."

I prop the phone against a pillow, making sure the shot is framed perfectly to capture Savvy's pelvis and nothing more, and then I slide two fingers deep inside Savvy's wetness and my thumb up her ass. And then, as my fingers begin to work her methodically, I kiss her plump lips. Suck her nipples. Whisper to her that she's gorgeous and sexy and turning me on. And that's all it takes. Within a few minutes, the girl is growling and writhing like she's been possessed by a demon.

"Oh, God," Savvy grits out. "Oh, my fucking God. Oh *fuck*." She makes a tortured sound, arches her back, whimpers...and then...*Nirvana*. Yet again, her deepest muscles begin rippling against my fingers inside her. But this time, even harder than the prior two times.

I'm dying to plunge myself inside Savvy and pound her without mercy. Of course, I am. But there's still one thing I want Derek to see before that. The video still recording, I lie on my back, grab Savvy's phone off the mattress, and hand it to her. "Climb aboard my face, baby," I choke out. "Make sure you get the ring in the shot."

Savvy doesn't hesitate. She climbs on top of my face and lowers her pussy onto my lips and I eat her out ravenously until, jackpot, her most intimate flesh begins rippling against my lips and tongue and fingers. I'm about to push her off me so I can lay her down and fuck her, but she surprises me by leaning forward over my torso and sucking me off like a woman possessed. So, of course, I do what comes naturally in this position: I treat myself to every square inch of her ass as she devours me.

Oh, God, I'm losing my mind. I haven't even fucked this girl yet, and I'm already having the best sex of my life. Holy shit. I thought I'd be showing *Savvy* what white-hot chemistry feels like tonight, but it turns out this girl is showing *me*.

When I can't take anymore of Savvy's mouth on me without losing it, I guide her firmly off me and onto her back, grab a condom from my bag, and get myself covered—faster than I ever have before—and then open her legs roughly with my thighs and plunge my throbbing cock inside her.

As I penetrate Savvy, we both moan with relief and excitement. And then I get to work. Oh, for the love of fuck, this feels good. I'm fucking her hard, grinding my hips with gusto—and Savvy is giving as good as she gets. She wraps her thighs around my torso and groans and pants into my ear. Her fingernails dig into my shoulders like she's hanging onto the edge of a cliff.

"Savvy," I choke out. "Oh, God. Savvy."

"No names," she says, barely able to get the words out.

"The camera's off."

"Aiden, Aiden, Aiden," comes her passionate reply. "Oh, God, *Aiden*." She drags her nails down my back, sending a bullet of pleasure into my dick, and I groan loudly and fuck her even harder, saying her name over and over again.

We're both shuddering, sweating, ferociously growling with desire. I kiss her deeply, desperately, losing my mind— and she grips me hard as I drive into her over and over again. Suddenly, out of nowhere, I'm jolted with a shock of energy the likes of which I've never felt before, as an electric current courses between us. I gasp in surprise and Savvy does too—both of us at the exact same time—and there's no doubt in my mind she's feeling the same lightning bolt I am. Pure unadulterated pleasure. Supernatural pleasure. *Ecstasy.*

With a loud moan, Savvy arches her back underneath me, digs her nails into my back *hard*, and comes. And when her internal muscles undulate around my cock, the sensation is so fucking good, I can't help releasing inside her with the most intense orgasm of my life.

Little white stars fill my vision. For a brief, blissful moment, as every cell in my body convulses with pleasure. I can't tell whose body is whose. Whose pleasure is whose. Whose heartbeat is whose. Finally, when the shockwaves end, I crumple on top of her, twitching with aftershocks and sweating like I've just run a full marathon.

"Holy fuck," I gasp out when my body finally goes quiet.

Savvy breathes deeply underneath me, and I feel her breasts press against my hard chest. "*Holy fuck*," she agrees.

For a long moment, we lie together, breathing hard, our sweat intermingling, our breathing in sync, our hearts pounding as one.

"I think I can safely say I've never experienced white-hot chemistry before this," Savvy deadpans after a long moment. And we both burst out laughing.

"Neither have I, apparently," I admit, rolling off her. "I thought I had, but obviously not."

"Seriously?"

"One hundred percent. That was hands down, no contest, far and away the best sex of my life."

"For me, too," she says.

I laugh and stroke her breast. "Yeah, I know, chicken girl. That goes without saying."

Savvy giggles and sighs happily. "So much for me going back to my safety zone after this, huh? I hope you're happy, Aiden Who Isn't Ugly. You've officially ruined me for anyone else. Thanks for nothing."

Savvy laughs, but I don't join her. Because, suddenly, visions of Savvy having sex with another guy are flooding me... and the idea makes me feel homicidal. *Fuck!* Of course, I don't want her muddling through ho-hum sex ever again. I want her to have white-hot, awesome sex from this day forward... *but only with me.* I realize I've got no right to feel that way. I know I just met this hot mess of a girl mere hours ago and that I'll never see her again after we get to Vegas tomorrow. Not to mention she's so far out of my league, it's not even funny. But lying here right now, what I'm honestly feeling is...a primal desire to stake my claim.

Savvy runs her hand through my hair. "Seriously, Aiden. That was beyond amazing. It was life-changing."

I look into her deep brown eyes and sigh. "For me, too."

She rolls onto her side and props her cheek on her palm. Her face is utterly beautiful in the moonlight. "I never would have believed my body could do what it did tonight. Thank you for showing me. I didn't think I was all that sexual a person. I thought I didn't care about sex."

"And now?"

She giggles. "Now I know I *love* sex." She bites her lower lip. "When it's done right."

My stomach clenches. "Good. Now you know."

She grins adorably. "Thank you."

"Don't thank me. This wasn't charity for me. Trust me."

"No, thank you for turning the second worst day of my entire life into one of the very best." She touches my cheek. "I know we're going to part ways tomorrow after we get to Vegas. I totally understand that. But I just want you to know, Aiden, I'll never forget tonight as long as I live."

CHAPTER SEVEN

AIDEN

Thursday, 3:22 a.m.

"Aiden," Savvy whispers, pulling me out of my dream. She presses her body against mine. Her skin is shockingly cold. "*Aiden*," she whispers again.

I jolt awake. "Holy shit."

She giggles. "I'm *freeeeeezing*."

"Yeah, I can feel that."

"I got up to use the bathroom and brush my teeth and guzzle a gallon of water, and now my teeth are chattering. The air conditioning is on full blast. Icicles are forming in here. Gimme your body heat. *Gah*."

Laughing, I wrap my arms around her and pull her into me—and when I surmise she's naked, and her nipples are rock hard, my dick begins tingling. "*Hello*," I say suggestively.

"*Hello*," she whispers, mimicking my tone. "Guess what?"

"What?"

"I'm sober now." She nuzzles the tip of her cold nose across my jawline. "And now I want to go back for seconds."

"No regrets about what we did in our drunken state?"

"Not a one. In fact, I just sent Derek all our mini-pornos."

"Seriously?"

"Yep. Every single one of them. My ruby ring is a star! *And guess what else?*" Her warm hand finds its way to my hard-on underneath the covers. She begins stroking me. "Sending those videos to Derek...feeling like I finally got to punch back for once in my life...*it turned me on like crazy.*"

I put my hand on Savvy's to stop her movement. "Hang on a sec, baby." *Shit.* I want nothing more than to fuck her again. But now that I'm completely sober, I feel the need to make things extra clear. "I'm having a blast with you, Savvy," I say. "Tonight's been one of the best of my life."

She pulls her hand off me. Clearly, she thinks I'm about to humiliate her in some way.

"Hey," I say softly. "Don't worry. Now that we're both sober, I just want to be clear this is a one-night thing. My life is a clusterfuck of epic proportions. As amazing as our chemistry has been, I still won't be able to hang out with you after we get to Vegas."

Her body language next to me is tight. "You've got a girlfriend."

"No. Nothing like that. It's the timing, Savvy. I met you at the worst possible time. You said you want a guy to be straight with you at all times, right up front, right? So I'm just making sure we're good."

"What's going on with you, Aiden? Why is this such a bad time in your life?"

I exhale. "I don't want to drag you into my mess. Just believe me when I say I'd pursue something with you beyond a one-night fling if I could. I truly would. I've never met anyone like you. Our connection is blowing my mind. But I just can't do it right now. I know casual sex isn't something you're accustomed to. I just want to make sure you're clear every step of the way."

"Maybe I could help you with whatever problem you're having."

"You can't help me."

"You're a fugitive from the law, aren't you? You're wanted by the FBI?"

"No. It's nothing like that." It's a true statement, technically. Yeah, I'm an ex-con, but I'm not currently wanted by any branch of law enforcement. I've done my time, and I'm a straight arrow these days. In fact, I haven't so much as jay-walked since I got out of the pen three years ago. I continue, "I've just got a personal emergency I need to handle. It's time-sensitive and fucked up, and I have to figure it out on my own. I can't even begin to think about trying to live a normal, happy life until I do that."

"Do you work for the mob? Are you a drug runner? Please tell me, Aiden. I might be able to help you."

I pause for a long moment, considering how much I want to tell her. "It's my father," I say tentatively. "He owes some money, and I'm the only one who can help him get it. That's really all I can say."

"He's in trouble with loan sharks?"

I sigh. *Jesus God, she's persistent.* "I don't want to talk about it, Savvy. Okay? *Please.*"

She's quiet for a long moment. And then she snuggles up close, slides her naked thigh over my hip and her palm to my naked ass, and sighs audibly. "All right. Thank you for making things clear. I admit I was starting to have fantasies of us having sex in my bed in LA."

Me too, I think. But, of course, I don't say it.

We lie in silence for a long moment, our limbs intertwined. I'm stroking her naked back. She's running her fingertips across my abs.

"Okay," she finally says. "If tonight is truly our one and only hurrah, then I say let's make our minutes count. Let's have another round of amazing sex."

Wordlessly, I pull her to me and kiss her and caress her until she's panting and moaning against me. When I know I've got her right where I want her, I reach between her legs and massage her hard, swollen tip. In no time flat, she's coming against my hand and moaning my name, and I'm losing my mind and wishing, so badly, I could do this to her beyond tonight. But I can't. Of course not.

My heart racing and my dick pulsing, I grab a condom off the nightstand, get myself covered, and sink myself inside her. Soon, we're on fire again, every bit as much as we were the first time. I thrust into her harder and harder, my body barreling toward release, until sweat is dripping down my back, and she's gasping for air and clawing at my shoulders, and my mind is not my own.

"Aiden," Savvy gasps out, her nails dragging down my back, her heart pounding with mine. "I'm... Oh, God." She arches her back forcefully, widens her legs, and comes so hard I feel liquid trickle against my balls. And that's it. I can't hang on. With a loud groan, I explode into her...so forcefully I'm suddenly seeing little white stars.

When our bodies quiet down, I roll off her and peel my condom off. My mind is racing. My heart aches. I suddenly feel an acute pang of regret. Of lost opportunity. Why'd I have to meet this incredible girl *now*?

"Do you feel that *thing* when we get going really good?" Savvy asks.

"That electricity?" I reply. "Yeah. It's crazy."

"It's insane. I got so turned on that time, I think I peed a little bit. Sorry."

"That wasn't pee." I explain the phenomenon of female ejaculation to her, and she marvels and gasps and expresses absolute shock. I rise up onto my elbow and look down at her pretty face in the moonlight and stroke her cheek with my thumb. "What the hell are you doing to me, Savannah Valentine?" I whisper.

Her features melt. She pulls me to her for a kiss. And the moment my lips meet hers, my chest aches with regret yet again. *Goddamnit, I don't want to say goodbye to this incredible girl tomorrow.* But I can't in good conscience *not* say goodbye to her. There's no umbrella big enough to protect her from the shitstorm that is my life.

But the thing is...

What if she's right about maybe being able to help me? Maybe I should tell her what's going on, just in case. She's smart about things I'm not. Maybe she'll have an idea.

No.

I'm being a dick to even think that way. Savvy is squeaky clean. Whether she's smart or not, I can't be selfish. I've got to keep her pristine.

And yet...

Fuck!

I want so badly to see where this thing between us might lead. What if my Plan A in Vegas works out for me, and I don't have to do Plan B on Saturday night? I could go to Savvy's reunion and fuck her all night long afterward... *No, Aiden.* You can't drag Savvy into your bullshit. You can't. And you can't give her false hope, either. Because the odds are high Plan A won't work out for me and I'll be forced to report for duty at the birthday party on Saturday night.

But what if I were to bare my soul to her, the same way she's done with me, and she still wants me? What if I can have my cake and eat it, too?

"I'm a felon," I whisper, out of nowhere, shocking myself.

Savvy stares at me, her eyes wide.

Shit. "Bank robbery," I continue, my chest tight. "I got out of prison three years ago. I served two years of a three-year sentence. I drove the getaway car for my father when he did the actual robberies. Two of them. I would have driven my father three times, but he never came out of the third bank." My heart is racing. Why am I telling her this? What the fuck am I doing? "I got out early for good behavior," I ramble on, unable to stop myself. "And I haven't had so much as a speeding ticket since I got out. I swear I've been on the straight and narrow since I got out three years ago, Savvy. But...yeah. I'm a felon." I press my lips together and wait, my heart thudding in my ears and my stomach turning somersaults.

Savvy blinks slowly, processing everything I've just said.

"Am I an idiot to be lying here with you? Are you going to steal from me? Harm me?"

My heart stops. "No, I'd never lay a pinky on you or any other woman. And I'm not going to steal from you, either. If I wanted to do that, I could have done it ten different times tonight. You left your purse with me when you went to the bathroom in the taco place, remember?"

She stares into my eyes in the moonlight for a long beat, her expression unreadable to me. "Did anyone get hurt during the bank robberies?"

"No. My dad never had a weapon. He just slipped the tellers a note. Tellers are trained to give up all the cash in their drawer in any kind of robbery, whether there's a weapon involved or not. Doing it that way limited his haul from any particular robbery to whatever happened to be in the particular teller's drawer. Usually, five to seven grand. But that was fine because the reason we were robbing banks in the first place was to help my father's brother. He needed money for medical treatments, and each treatment cost around five grand."

"Medical treatments for what?"

"For brain cancer. My Uncle Jimmy was my father's younger brother—my father's only family before I knocked on his door at fourteen. Dad and Jimmy grew up together in foster care. So when Jimmy got sick and needed money, Dad decided to do whatever he had to do. He tried everything he could to get the money Jimmy needed legally, but nothing panned out. So, finally, Dad was like, 'Fuck it. I'll rob some fucking banks, then.'"

"I'm not impressed your father involved his teenage son

in his plan."

"He didn't want me to help him. He refused at first. But I knew he'd get caught if he didn't have a quick getaway, and the most important thing was helping Jimmy. That was more important to both of us than the risk."

"Did your father serve his time at the same prison as you?"

"No. We were separated. And he served five years, not two. He had three charges against him, unlike me. The actual robberies plus an attempt. Plus, my father had some priors, unlike me. Stupid shit from when he was younger. He got out of prison a couple months ago."

"And he's already in trouble?"

"Pretty sure I mentioned my dad's a royal fuck-up."

"And what about Jimmy?"

"He died a few months after Dad and I got arrested."

"I'm sorry."

"It wasn't really my loss. It was my dad's. He was decimated."

Savvy inches closer to me and strokes my arm...and every molecule in my body exalts at her touch. Does this mean she's not scared of me? That, at least for tonight, in her bed, she accepts me for who I am? For a long moment, I lie quietly with Savvy, reveling in her touch, my heart racing, waiting for her to talk again.

Finally, Savvy says, "Was prison horrible?"

"Yes, but not in the ways you're probably thinking. In movies, they always show guys covering their assholes at every turn, afraid to shower or bend down. But it's not like that. Guys don't get raped in prison the way they show in movies. I mean, they *do* get raped, but not nearly as much as people think. Most sex in prison is consensual. Actually, most of the time, it's with guards."

She grimaces. "Did you have sex with guards?"

"No. I had sex with nobody but me. I kept to myself the whole two years."

She studies my face.

"It's true."

"Were you scared?"

"Yes. But not too much. As strange as it sounds, prisoners have a strong moral code. If you're in there for hurting a woman or child, then good luck. You're gonna get fucked up the ass and beaten to a pulp and maybe a lot worse. But if you robbed banks with your father to get money for your sick uncle's chemo, they pretty much leave you alone. I was especially golden because once I'd earned the privilege of going to the rec room each week, I fell into teaching guitar to a bunch of pretty scary dudes. One of them made it known I was his friend. After that, everyone pretty much left me alone. I mean, yeah, things got dicey sometimes. Several times, I shit a brick the size of Nebraska. But most of the time, prison was just painfully boring. The hardest part was the head-game of it all. Trying to survive being locked up without going crazy. I wouldn't have minded it so much if I'd had access to a guitar or piano more than a few hours a week. If I could have made music twenty-four-seven while locked up, I would have been just fine."

"So what did you do to pass the time, if you couldn't make music?"

"I worked out."

"That explains it."

"I also had a job. I was assigned to cleaning toilets. Believe it or not, that was a great job for me because I was alone. And that meant I could think and write songs in my head as I worked. I came out of prison with three full albums' worth of songs in my head. I also figured out I'm dyslexic in prison. That was a good thing."

"How did you figure that out?"

"This woman doing a research study about dyslexia came to the prison to find test subjects. Get this—twenty percent of the general population has dyslexia, but *forty-eight* percent of the prison population has it."

"Wow."

"So word got out this woman was interviewing guys to see if they were dyslexic. And I was like, well, I'm not dyslexic, obviously—I'm just an idiot. But, hey, everyone says she's got cookies, so I'll talk to her."

Savvy chuckles.

"And the minute she started asking me questions, she knew. She was like, 'Aiden, honey, you're textbook.'"

"Oh, my gosh."

"My mind was blown. Before that moment, I truly thought I was stupid. But it turns out I'm not. I'm actually really smart."

"Of course, you are. I could have told you that, just from talking to you."

"I always knew I was smart about life and music and people," I say. "But when it came to school stuff—the stuff that people typically measure to tell if you're smart—I always felt like the stupidest guy in every room. And Gramps was always like, 'I was terrible in school, too. All you need is music and you'll be fine, Aidy.' So I didn't worry about it."

"I wonder if your grandfather was dyslexic, too?"

"Oh, yeah. In retrospect, I have no doubt he was. But at the time, all I knew was that, when I was playing music, I felt like a genius. I could write bass lines to go with guitar lines to go with piano lines, all in my head. But ask me to do a standardized reading comprehension test, and I couldn't do it."

"Was your dyslexia treated in prison, or just diagnosed?"

"Treatment was part of the gig. The reward for participating in the research study. Well, that and cookies."

Savvy laughs.

"It was awesome. I met with Dr. Finelli—the woman doing the research project—twice a week for a year. That was the max allowed, and I took full advantage. She even came to visit me sometimes during visiting hours to help me, just because she cared about me. And once those letters and numbers started unscrambling inside my brain, I was a new man. I started reading everything I could get my hands on. Classics. Mysteries. Music biographies. Music theory. I was in prison, yeah. And dying to play my guitar. But my mind finally felt free."

Savvy lifts her head from my chest and beams a beautiful smile at me. "I just got goose bumps, Aiden."

We share a smile.

"Thank you for telling me all of this."

"Thank you for not kicking me out of your bed after hearing the truth about me."

"Of course not."

"Are you still willing to drive me to Vegas tomorrow?" I ask.

"Of course." She drags the pad of her fingertip across my lower lip. "Frankly, it turns me on to find out I've slept with an actual *felon*. Before you, I thought sleeping with a 'bad boy' meant sleeping with a guy who'd gotten an A minus in calculus."

I laugh.

Savvy continues. "I'd rather be lying here with you—an honest felon—than a dude with no criminal history who lies shamelessly to my face to get me into bed."

My heart is leaping. "I've had a fantastic time with you," I whisper. "I'll never forget tonight."

"Same," she whispers. "You're imprinted on my heart forever."

CHAPTER EIGHT

AIDEN

Thursday, 9:13 a.m.

I open my eyes to find Savvy sitting at a small table across the room, showered and dressed and clacking on the keyboard of a laptop. Her brow is furrowed. Her lips are pursed. *She's in the zone.* And she looks sexy as hell.

"Good morning, Savvy Who Isn't Savvy," I say, folding my arms behind my head and smiling at her.

Savvy looks up, and her pretty face lights up. "Good morning, Aiden Who Isn't Ugly. How are you feeling?"

"Good. Not hung over at all. You?"

"Good. A teeny bit hung over, but not too bad. I drank a ton of water and took some ibuprofen in the middle of the night, thankfully."

"Whatcha doing? You look like you're plotting something diabolical."

"Nothing too exciting. I'm reading a report on the background check I ran on you, Aiden *MacAllister*. And I'm thrilled to report everything you told me last night checks out."

I can't breathe. "You're in law enforcement? You said you're an accountant."

Savvy puts her elbows on the table and grins. "I'm not in law enforcement. And I never said I'm an accountant. You assumed that. I said the firm where I worked was a full-service accounting and finance firm with lots of different divisions, including cybersecurity, where I worked."

"You're a hacker?"

"Correct. But not in the way most people use that word. I'm purely white hat preventative. My job is—or *was*, up until yesterday—to find all the ways corporate clients might be vulnerable to hacking so I could protect them. In other words, I found the holes so I could plug them up." She grins adorably.

"Impressive. So, tell me, Little Miss Hacker... What cyber voodoo magic did you use to lead you to my last name? I'm positive I never mentioned it to you last night."

"You didn't."

"So what did you do? Take note of every little bread crumb I babbled to you last night—about Nashville and my grandfather and my mom's tour bus crash and my criminal record—and then put it all together and connect the dots?"

"Yes. That's exactly what I did. Brilliant, huh?"

"Genius."

"Well, either that or I peeked at your driver's license while you were sleeping."

"Ah, the ol' peek-at-the-license maneuver," I manage to say, doing my best to keep my voice relaxed. *What else did Savvy see when she was poking around in my backpack?* "So did you riffle through my entire backpack or just grab my wallet and peek at my license?"

Savvy flashes me a flirtatious smile. "I just grabbed your

wallet. Why? Did I miss seeing a big ol' brick of cocaine at the bottom of your backpack? Are you a drug mule for a Mexican cartel?"

The playful look on Savvy's face tells me she genuinely has no idea there's an envelope filled with twenty-five grand in cash sitting in a side compartment of my backpack.

I raise three fingers into a Boy Scout pledge. "I'm not a drug mule. I promise. The only drug in my backpack is ibuprofen. I was just curious what kinds of information a brainiac hacker like yourself uses to run a background check."

"I had everything I needed right here." She taps her computer.

I sigh with relief. I have zero desire to explain that twenty-five grand to her. "So what did Derek the Douchebag say about all the homemade porn you sent him?"

"He hasn't responded yet. But that's not unexpected, seeing as how I chucked his phone off the top of a mountain yesterday. He probably hasn't seen the videos quite yet."

"You're seriously not freaking out you sent them to him?"

"Why should I? Thanks to your suggestion, the world won't know it's me fucking that tattooed hottie in the videos. Honestly, I'm elated I sent those videos to Derek. I'm a woman who's all out of fucks to give."

I laugh. "Or as my grandfather used to say, 'Your give-a-shitter done broke.'"

Savvy whoops. "Oh, I *love* that. *My give-a-shitter done broke.* Yup. That's exactly right." She bites her lip and flashes me a sexy look. "So, hey, you want to watch our videos? I watched them this morning while you were still sleeping, and I must say, I enjoyed them."

I pat the bed next to me. "Hell yeah."

Smiling from ear to ear, Savvy grabs her phone and joins me in the bed and we begin watching our videos. But by the time we get to the video of Savvy sitting on my face, we're both far too turned on to watch ourselves any longer...and, quickly, life begins furiously imitating art.

CHAPTER NINE

SAVANNAH

Aiden and I are sitting across from each other at a diner along the route to Las Vegas. And, the same way I've been doing all morning since we left the motel, I'm trying to muster the courage to say something in particular to him.

"How's your food?" I ask, indicating the omelet in front of him. But, damn it, asking Aiden about his food isn't what I've been dying to talk to him about.

"It's great," Aiden replies. "How's yours?"

"Great," I say. I take a bite of my food. And then a sip of my coffee. And clear my throat. "Thanks so much for playing me those songs in the car. I loved hearing you talk about your grandfather's contributions to music history." *Damn.* That wasn't the thing I've been dying to say to Aiden, either, although I did, in fact, love hearing the songs Aiden played me in the car—songs featuring Ernie "Mac" MacAllister on guitar. And even more so, I loved hearing Aiden rhapsodize about his grandfather's guitar playing on the songs.

"You sure I didn't bore the hell out of you?" Aiden says.

"Are you kidding? You gave me goose bumps at least ten times."

Aiden beams a huge smile at me and then takes a bite of his food.

Crap. I'm running out of time to make this suggestion. I need to just spit it out. "So, hey, Aiden, I was thinking." Oh, God, my heart is racing. "What if I were to buy you out of your contract?"

Aiden stares at me blankly.

I continue. "What if I were to pay you whatever you'll be getting to perform at that birthday party in Vegas on Saturday night? It'd be the best of both worlds. You'd be able to come to my reunion and still be able to earn the exact same amount of money. Saturday is still two days away. Plenty of time for the party organizer to find someone else to play, especially in a city like Vegas where..." I trail off. Aiden looks uncomfortable. And that's making me realize I must have pulled another Savvy. Misread the nonverbal cues. Taken a person's words literally when they were simply being polite. I look down at my hands. "Oh. I just realized you only said that thing about my reunion to be nice, and I took you literally. Sorry."

"Savvy, no," Aiden says sharply. "Look at me."

I look up from my hands, my heart pounding.

"I told you the truth. If I could go with you to your reunion on Saturday night, I would. But it's not possible. And it's a moot point anyway because you can't possibly afford to buy me out of my contract."

I sigh. "Maybe I could. How much could they possibly be paying you? A grand? I looked up the going rate for solo musicians on this party website and it said—"

"Twenty-five grand."

My heart stops. I shut my mouth and blink several times in rapid succession like a lizard on a rock, but I can't make sense of the words I've just heard. "What?"

"I'm getting paid twenty-five grand."

I can't fathom how that's possible. *Aiden is getting paid twenty-five grand to sing and play his acoustic guitar at a birthday party?* Is he an undercover rock star? Maybe some big country star I've never heard of because I don't typically listen to that kind of music? But, no, that can't be. When I scoured the internet for information about Aiden MacAllister, nothing came up that even remotely suggested Aiden could command *twenty-five grand* to play his guitar at a freaking birthday party, whether in Sin City or anywhere else. Plus, hold up. Didn't Aiden tell me his weekly gig at that brunch place in Silver Lake is by far his best-paying gig? Didn't he say he can't pay his bills from music alone? Does. Not. Compute.

"But...you said you have to have a day job because music doesn't pay your bills," I say. "Twenty-five grand won't pay your bills? Do you have a coke habit or something?"

Aiden shakes his head. "No, I don't have a coke habit. I don't do drugs."

"What aren't you telling me?" I whisper, my stomach clenching. I wrap my arms around my torso, girding myself for whatever bomb Aiden is about to drop on me. "Whatever you're hiding from me, tell me, Aiden. Tell me now."

Aiden leans back in his chair. He rubs his face. "I'm so sorry, Savvy. I—"

"Refills?" the waitress chirps, appearing out of nowhere with a coffee pot.

We both shake our heads, and she leaves. And the minute she's gone, I lean forward, my cheeks burning.

"Whatever you're about to say to me, make sure it contains exactly zero lies," I whisper. "I'm done being lied to, Aiden, by anyone, ever again. If you lie to me, be prepared to get another ride to Vegas from here."

Aiden looks tortured. He bites his cheek, but he remains mute. Clearly, he's choosing his words carefully.

"Are you even a musician?" I whisper.

"Of course." He motions to his music-themed tattoos. "Or else I'm a fucking psychopath."

"Are you a fucking psychopath?"

"No. I'm perfectly sane."

"Just tell me what's going on. Please."

He exhales a long breath. "I didn't lie to you, okay? That's the most important thing you need to know. I told you I'm a musician and that I'm working on Saturday night at a birthday party—both true. But I never said I'm playing *music* at that birthday party. You connected those dots on your own." He grimaces. "And...I didn't correct you."

"You haven't been hired to play music at the birthday party?"

He shakes his head.

I cross my arms over my chest. "What did they hire you to do?"

He looks like he wants to throw up.

"You're doing something illegal, aren't you? I was right this morning. You're a drug mule. You work for a cartel."

He rolls his eyes. "I'm not a drug mule, Savvy. This has

nothing to do with drugs." He sighs. "But, yes, it's something illegal. But only *technically*. It's a victimless crime." He grimaces again and mutters, "Unless you count *me*." When I look at him blankly, he takes a deep breath and speaks on his exhale. "I'm attending the party as the birthday girl's...date. I'm her birthday present to herself."

Shock. Repulsion. *Jealousy*. Those are the emotions instantly slamming into me in full force. I slam my fist on the table and lean forward, my cheeks blazing hot. "*You're an escort?*"

Aiden nods.

"*A twenty-five-thousand-dollar escort?*"

"Yes."

I stare at him, expecting him to elaborate, but he doesn't. "Well, are you a paid escort as in 'fake boyfriend' or as in '*gigolo*'?"

Aiden cringes sharply at my last word, telling me the answer to my question is the latter option.

I put my hand to my mouth. "No."

He nods slowly, a look of pure nausea on his face.

"You're getting paid twenty-five thousand dollars to have sex with the birthday girl?"

He looks down at the table. "I'm hoping it won't come to that. But, yes."

I feel physically ill. Duped. Pissed. *Stupid*. "What do you mean you're hoping it won't come to that?"

He doesn't reply.

I wait.

Still nothing.

"So that's your day job, then?" I ask. "*Fucking?* You lied to me about working construction? You're actually some kind of con artist!"

Aiden snaps his head up and levels me with blazing blue eyes that physically jolt me. "No, I'm not a con artist. And I'm not a liar. I didn't lie to you, Savvy. Other than when I didn't correct your assumption about what I'd be doing at the birthday party, I've been completely honest with you. More honest with you than anyone, ever, actually. Not sure why. When I said I've never done anything like this before, that was true. When I said I'm hoping I won't have to do it now, that was true, too. Selling myself to someone I don't want to fuck is most definitely my Plan B. I'll do it if I have to do it simply because I'm in a bad situation and my father needs the money, but I'm genuinely hoping it won't come to that. I know the world assumes men will happily fuck anyone at all, but it's not true. At least, not for me. I don't fuck unless I'm feeling it. Like I told you, if I'm not feeling it, I'd rather be alone with my guitar, my hand, and a bottle of lube. But I might not have a choice in this instance, so fuck it, I'll do whatever I have to do."

His chest is heaving. His eyes are on fire. His jaw is tight. And God help me, I believe every word he just said to me. I could be wrong—God knows I could, knowing me. But the look on Aiden's face tells me he's baring his soul to me. "What's going on, Aiden?" I ask. "What do you mean it's your Plan B? What do you mean you're in a bad situation? Is your father in some sort of trouble? Does he owe money to loan sharks?"

"I don't want to get you involved, Savvy."

"Too late."

"It's not too late. When we get to Vegas, I'm going to say goodbye to you for your own good. I'll do my thing, whatever I have to do, and keep you the fuck out of this. I shouldn't have said anything to you. I just..." He shakes his head and looks down. "I just can't get you involved."

I stare at him for a long moment. "What do you mean sleeping with the birthday girl is Plan B? What's Plan A?"

He sighs. "There's something I'm going to do when I get to Vegas. But I can't guarantee it will work. Which means I can't guarantee I won't have to follow through with the job with the birthday girl—which is why I think it's best we say goodbye when we get to Vegas. Not only do I not want to drag you into this, I selfishly don't want to have to see the look in your eye if I wind up stringing you along and giving you hope and then having to report for duty with the birthday girl, regardless. The more time we spend together, the more attached we're going to become. That much is clear to me. And if it turns out I have no choice but to shut my eyes and give the birthday girl what she wants, I don't want to break your heart." He looks down again. "Or mine."

My heart lurches into my throat. "You need to tell me everything right now."

"I don't want to get you involved."

"Jesus Christ." I grunt with frustration. "Enough with that."

He doesn't speak.

"Just tell me who the hell is this birthday girl?" I bellow. "I mean, seriously! What self-respecting woman would pay a guy twenty-five grand to sleep with her, when he has no desire to do it? Is she some spoiled brat who saw you playing at that brunch place in Silver Lake? Did she tell her daddy she saw the most gorgeous man in the world, and she just had to—"

"She's not a girl," Aiden says. "She's a full-grown woman. I used the phrase 'birthday *girl*' as a figure of speech. She's throwing herself a fiftieth birthday party on Saturday night."

I've been rendered speechless.

Aiden continues, "Her name is Regina. She's an old friend of my father's. She's been covertly hitting on me since I was sixteen years old. I've always brushed her off. Ignored her. Left the room. I've never told a soul about her bullshit. But then my father called me Wednesday morning, freaking the fuck out, telling me he needs money, and I felt like I had no other option but to call Regina and beg her to help me."

"It's loan sharks, right? I know it is. Just tell me."

Aiden exhales. "Yes. But I really didn't want to get you involved with this, Savvy. You're squeaky clean."

"Too late. I'm involved. Now tell me everything. *Right fucking now.*"

He closes his eyes and sighs.

"If this situation weren't hanging over your head, would you want to say goodbye to me in Vegas?" I ask.

He opens his eyes. "No."

"Well, I don't want to say goodbye to you, either. So tell me everything so maybe, just maybe, I can help you with this mess."

He hesitates.

"Goddamnit, Aiden! Not telling me is the same thing as lying to me, as far as I'm concerned. If you want to have any sliver of a chance with me, then tell me everything right now."

He throws up his hands. "I don't have a sliver of a chance with you, regardless. Don't you understand? If it weren't for this shitstorm, I'd still be dreaming to get with a girl like you. You're this...brainiac college graduate corporate America Girl Scout. And I'm..." He lowers his head. "Not a guy a girl like you would bring home to meet the parents."

I stare at his bowed head for a very long moment. How is it possible I feel so moved by this man, this quickly? How is it possible my heart feels like it's physically straining for him? "Okay, first off, fuck everything you just said. It's total bullshit. Aiden, look at me."

He lifts his head.

"Fuck that 'We don't fit together' bullshit. It's stupid and I categorically reject it. But there's no time to have a therapy session over that right now. What matters is you're in a bad situation, and your father needs money, and you're willing to sacrifice yourself to help him—*and I want to help you*. That's all that matters right now."

He nods.

I continue, "Whether we're going to see each other ever again after today or not, I want to help you, regardless. I don't expect anything from you, okay? You won't be obligated to me if I help you. Just let me help you, if I can, simply because I want to do it."

He nods. "Thank you."

"Tell me what's going on. Tell me all of it."

Aiden considers my plea for a long moment. Finally, he sighs and says, "My dad owes fifty grand to some loan sharks, and they're holding him as collateral in a motel in Henderson. If he doesn't pay them what he owes by Sunday night, they're gonna shoot him in the head. He called me on Wednesday around three in the morning from the motel where he's being held, totally freaking out. I told him not to worry, that I'd handle everything. So then I hung up and called Regina—the birthday girl—because she's the only rich person I know. She used to hang out with my dad off and on before he went to prison five years ago. I begged her for the fifty grand my father needs. I told her I'd do anything. Remodel her kitchen. *Anything*." He rolls his eyes. "It didn't even occur to me she'd demand to fuck me. Yeah, she used to hit on me all the time, but I didn't think she was such a monster that she'd..." He sighs and shakes his head. "I couldn't believe my ears, Savvy. I couldn't believe it. I begged her for the full fifty, but twenty-five was as high as she'd go." He sighs. "So I said fine."

I'm quaking with rage. "Jesus Christ." I rub my forehead. "Is there an agreement on how many hours you're supposed to spend with her on Saturday night? Does she expect you to spend the *entire* night with her?"

"Actually, she expects me to spend a full *forty-eight hours* with her. The job starts tomorrow at noon and ends Sunday at noon."

I gasp. "*No*. You can't do this, Aiden. Some things are worth more than money."

His face ignites. He leans forward sharply, his face ablaze. "You think I don't know that, Savvy? You think I don't know she'll be buying my integrity—my very soul—along with my cock? Of course, I know that. Give me some fucking credit.

But normal rules of morality and decency don't apply here. Not when my dad's life is at stake. He's not going to get a *figurative* bullet in his brain. They're going to *kill* him. I *literally* need fifty grand to save my father's *life* and, by God, I'm gonna get that fifty grand, if it's the last thing I do. I wish my father and I were the kind of people who could get a loan from a bank, but we're not. I wish we had family to turn to, but we don't. It's just me and him and nobody else. So, fuck it, I'll do whatever I have to do to save him because he's mine and I'm his, and there's no choice in the matter." He looks around, clearly worried someone will overhear him. He leans forward again and whispers, "You think I *want* to fuck her? I don't. I hate that woman. I *hate* her. I grew up *aching* to have a mom. That's all I ever wanted. To have a mother to love me and take care of me like the other kids had. And then at sixteen I met my dad's rich fuck buddy, and for a split second I was thinking she might become kind of like a mom. I thought she was being extra nice to me because she was feeling *maternal* toward me." He scoffs. "I was thinking she might actually care about me the way I'd been aching my whole life for a woman to do." His face darkens. "And then it turned out she just wanted to fuck me."

"Oh, Aiden."

"Honestly, if it comes down to it, and I have to follow through with fucking that woman—for forty-eight fucking hours, no less—I'm sincerely not sure how I'll physically manage it, no matter what's at stake. I figure I'll just snort every line of coke she offers me and pop ten Viagras and close my eyes. But I swear to God, I'll do whatever has to be done, come hell or high water. I'll get blitzed out of my mind and do it, Savvy, my integrity be damned, because I can't lose my father." Emotion grips his face. "I owe him my life. And he's all I've got left."

I remain silent for a long moment, simply because I'm overwhelmed by the torrent of emotion I'm feeling. Finally, I gather myself and say, "You have until Sunday night to get the fifty grand?"

Aiden nods. "Sunday at eight. Originally, my father owed fifty-eight grand, and they were gonna kill him on Wednesday night. But I wired them every penny of my life's savings—just about eight grand—on Wednesday morning, and they agreed to give him an extension to come up with the rest. But if I don't bring them the money by Sunday at eight, and not a minute later, they'll kill him."

I feel like crying. Aiden has already had enough loss and heartbreak and suffering in his life. He doesn't need *this*, too. "What is your—?"

"Refills?" the waitress asks, appearing at the edge of the table, holding a coffee pot.

"Just our bill, please," Aiden says politely. "Thanks."

The woman briefly searches the pocket in her apron and pulls out our check. "Here you go. Was everything okay?"

"It was great," Aiden says. He hands her twenty-five bucks without looking at the bill. "Keep the change."

The waitress looks at the cash in her hand and smiles. "Thanks so much. Have a great day."

"You, too," Aiden says calmly.

The waitress leaves.

"Let me pay you back for breakfast," I say. "You paid for

drinks and food last night, too. You shouldn't be paying for anything. You need every dollar right now."

Aiden scoffs. "Sweetheart, when a dude's got to come up with seventy-five grand in three days, paying for his girl's drinks and food is the least of his worries."

"*Seventy-five* grand?" I blurt. "But this whole time you've been saying your dad owes *fifty*."

"Oh. Yeah. He does. But I need to come up with a total of seventy-five grand."

I feel like my head is going to explode. "Why?"

Aiden stands and wearily puts his hand out to me. "Come on, chicken girl. I'll tell you the whole fucked-up story as we drive."

CHAPTER TEN

SAVANNAH

As Aiden and I settle into my car in the parking lot, I suddenly lose my stiff upper lip. "I'm not ready to drive to Vegas just yet," I blurt. I drop my car keys into my drink holder in the console and put my hands over my face. "Not if it means saying goodbye to you when we get there."

Aiden sighs. He touches my shoulder. "Savvy."

I drop my hands and look at him with pleading eyes. "I know you have to take care of the situation with your dad when you get there. I get it. But I don't know why that means we have to say goodbye forever. Do you want to say goodbye to me in a couple hours, Aiden? Please answer me with brutal honesty. It's a moot point if you're not feeling what I am."

Aiden swallows hard. He looks positively stricken. "No, I told you honestly before, I don't want to say goodbye to you. Can't you tell how I'm feeling? Isn't it written all over my face? But it doesn't matter. I'm not getting you involved in this shit. Besides, the way we feel about each other will be a moot point if I wind up reporting for duty with Regina. If that happens, you won't want to see me afterward. You won't respect me anymore."

I let that hang in the air for a moment, not sure how to respond. Honestly, I think he's right about that. *Shit.*

"Don't you understand?" Aiden says, his eyes flashing. "When I get to Vegas, I'm going to do *whatever* I have to do to save my dad. *Whatever that is.* Even if that means losing my shot with you. And, frankly, if I fuck Regina, I won't *deserve* your respect anymore. I wouldn't want to pursue you because I'd know you could do a whole lot better." He looks out the passenger window at the parking lot. "So I'd rather just say goodbye to you today. Part ways when you still think I'm some kind of Prince Charming. If I wind up selling myself to Regina, then I don't want to have to see the way you look at me when you find out."

"But what if you don't sell yourself to Regina?"

He turns away from the window to look at me with burning blue eyes. "And how would I maneuver that, Savvy? Should I agree to give you a call if I *don't* fuck Regina? Is that what you want?"

I shrug. Why is he making that sound like a weird idea?

He continues. "Think about it. What happens when I don't call you? You'll know what I did. You'll lie in bed after that, imagining me fucking her. And I'll lie in bed after that, thinking about you waiting by the phone for that call that never came. I'll imagine the look on your face the moment you realized I must have fucked her." His Adam's apple bobs. His torment is palpable. "I'd rather you not know, to be honest. I'd rather say goodbye now and let you wonder, rather than know. Because, truthfully, the chances are really slim my Plan A is going to work out. If I had a good shot of it panning out, yeah,

I'd stick to you like glue because you're the greatest girl I've ever met. But I don't have a good shot at my Plan A working out. I just don't."

I stare at his beautiful face for a long beat. His beautiful, earnest, heartbreaking face. "What is this Plan A of yours?" I say. "Tell me about it. Maybe I can help you make it work."

He leans back in his seat and closes his eyes. "Savvy, I never intended to get you involved in this shit."

I sigh.

"Can we just drive?" he asks weakly. "I've got to get to Vegas. I'm freaking the fuck out."

I pick up my keyring from the console and slide the correct key into the ignition. But I stop short before turning the engine over. "Please tell me if this is pathetic, but I want to be with you one last time." I look at him. "Let's find a back road somewhere and park. If we're truly going to say goodbye to each other when we get to Vegas, then I want to feel that crazy electricity with you once more." I swallow hard as emotion rises up inside me. "Because I'm not convinced I'll feel anything quite like it again."

Aiden touches my arm. "Aw, Savvy. I'm so sorry. I never meant for feelings to get involved here. This was supposed to be fun. A brief distraction from the shitstorm. Nothing but fun and an easy ride to Vegas." He leans back in his chair and closes his eyes. "Fuck."

I wait for a long moment and finally say, "One more time. If you want that, too."

Aiden opens his eyes and shoots me a heartbreaking half-smile. "Yeah. Of course, I want that, too. I can't imagine I'm ever gonna feel this kind of spark again, either."

My heart physically hurting, I nod and turn the ignition over. "But fair warning? When we hit the road again, I'm going to demand you tell me everything about your Plan A. Because if there's any way at all for me to help you, then I'm sure as hell going to do it."

CHAPTER ELEVEN

SAVANNAH

I don't want an inch of separation between us. I want all of him. Every inch. I hitch my legs up higher around Aiden's thrusting body, as high as I can manage in the cramped space of my backseat, trying to coax him into the farthest recesses of my body, and he responds by guiding my thighs to his shoulders and grinding himself into me with breathtaking fervor. In short order, my feet are whacking against the ceiling of my SUV. My head is banging against the side interior. And my innermost muscles have never felt this good in all my life.

Aiden growls my name as he thrusts, his voice husky with need and passion and desperation, and that's all I need for my body to release with an orgasm so pleasurable, it makes my eyes water.

"Get on top," Aiden barks out.

"We're like sardines in here."

"I want to get a video of your face. I want to remember the way you look when you come. It'd just be for me. I'll never show anybody."

I should say no. I know I should. But I don't. I say yes. Because trusting him completely is turning me on.

We rearrange ourselves indelicately, ridiculously, until I'm somehow on top of Aiden and riding him like a madwoman in the cramped back seat. And I must admit, once we're in position and Aiden is grabbing my ass with one hand and recording me with the other—all while looking up at me like I'm a wet dream—my body responds in a whole new way.

"You make me want to be worthy of you," Aiden whispers as I ride him furiously. He sits up and sucks on my nipple *hard*—so hard, so ferociously, I yelp like I've just touched a hot stove. He buries his face in my breasts, and I throw my head back, and it knocks against the ceiling of the car. Our movement becomes wild. Crazy. Intense. We're both gritting out words of passion. Urgency. *Desperation*. Aiden positions his phone to record my face while massaging my clit with his free hand. He tells me I'm beautiful. That he's going to look at this video of me every night for the rest of his life...and I lose my freaking mind. An orgasm of such force rips through me, I press my palms against the ceiling of the car to steady myself and howl at the top of my lungs.

"Fuck," Aiden blurts.

He drops the phone and comes inside me forcefully, and I flop forward, moaning and breathing hard.

Finally, we're both quiet. Covered in sweat. Panting.

I lift my head and cup his jawline in my palm. "You're not going to be her boy toy," I declare firmly. And, as far as I'm concerned, it's a nonnegotiable statement. "I don't know what Plan A is or how I'm going to help you with it, but, by God, I will. I'm smart, Aiden. *Really* smart. I'm going to help you figure out a solution to your problem, and you're not going to report for duty tomorrow. And that's final."

He looks bereft. "I know you're smart, Savvy. Ten times smarter than me. But it's not smarts I need, baby. It's luck. Lady luck."

"I knew it! Plan A is *gambling*?"

"Yes."

"Your big plan is to pay off a *gambling* debt by *gambling*?"

He makes an adorable face. "Ingenious, right?"

"Goddamnit," I mutter. I lean forward and put my forehead on his shoulder. No wonder Aiden has felt so hopeless about his Plan A working out. He said he needs *seventy-five* grand for some reason, not fifty. How could he possibly hope to win that much money from a casino, unless his seed money is at least, I don't know, twenty grand? No wonder he's willing to sell himself to Regina for twenty-five grand!

"Savvy?" he whispers. "What are you thinking?"

I lift my head. "I'm thinking it's time for you to tell me why you need seventy-five grand."

CHAPTER TWELVE

SAVANNAH

"You've got twenty-five grand *in cash* sitting in your backpack?" I ask, my eyes wide. I peel my attention off the highway and look at Aiden in my passenger seat. "That's an insane amount of cash to be carrying around in a freaking backpack, Aiden."

"I know. I've had a stomach ache since I walked out of the bank with it yesterday morning."

I grip the steering wheel. "And that guy at the museum said he'd *for sure* let you buy your grandfather's guitar back if you show up there Monday with the full twenty-five grand?"

"I've got it in writing," Aiden says. "If I show up with the full twenty-five grand before the museum's closing time on Monday, they're contractually obligated to return Betty to me. If I don't show up with the cash before the deadline, then she'll become theirs, and there's nothing I can do about it 'til the end of time."

"You call your grandfather's guitar Betty?"

Aiden shoots me a breathtaking smile from the passenger seat. "That's what Gramps always called that particular guitar. It was his all-time favorite. The love of his life."

"Your grandfather was a real character, wasn't he?"

"He was definitely one of a kind."

Oh, this boy. His face right now is making my heart burst. "I'm so glad you thought to negotiate a buyback period with the museum," I say. "That was a stroke of brilliance."

"A stroke of brilliance born of desperation," he replies. "I love Betty as much as Gramps did. Probably more, since it's all I've got left of him. I never in a million years thought I'd sell her for any amount, let alone a paltry twenty-five grand." He sighs. "But my father's life is worth more to me than any guitar. Even Betty."

My heart pangs for probably the twentieth time since Aiden started telling me his story—which, in summary, is this: When Ernie "Mac" MacAllister passed away ten years ago, he left his beloved fourteen-year-old grandson his most-treasured possession—the electric guitar he'd played on countless hit records over the decades. Of course, Aiden cherished that guitar for sentimental reasons, but he also knew it had objective value, too. Not only because his esteemed grandfather had played it on so many hit records, but also because his grandfather had made a habit of collecting signatures on the face of his guitar over the years—signatures of the sometimes iconic and beloved artists with whom Mac had played.

"Did you shop the guitar around to a bunch of museums?" I ask. "Maybe you could have gotten more than twenty-five grand."

"There was no time for that," Aiden says. "I knew that particular museum would pay good money for it, so that's where I went."

"How'd you know they'd buy it? Did they appraise it for you at some point?"

"No, I never even thought to get Betty appraised because I was never planning to sell her at any price. I knew that particular museum would buy the guitar because, about a year ago, I was playing a gig with a band in a bar, and this guy started chatting me up on our break. As it turned out, the guy was the museum's curator, and he offered me fifteen grand on the spot. Of course, I turned him down and told him Betty wasn't for sale at any price. But he goes, 'Well, if you change your mind, come down to see me at the museum any weekday. No appointment necessary. I'll cut you a check for fifteen grand on the spot.' So when I got off the phone with Regina, I hauled my ass straight over there."

"I'm impressed you were able to talk the museum guy up from fifteen grand."

"I tried to get him to the full fifty. The same as I tried with Regina. But twenty-five was the highest the guy would go."

"So you're going to try to parlay the twenty-five grand from the guitar into seventy-five so you can pay off your dad's debt *and* buy the guitar back from the museum?"

"Exactly."

"What game are you planning to play in the casino?"

"Roulette. I'm gonna put it all on black, baby."

"Twice? Because even if you win your first bet, you'll only have fifty grand at that point. Enough to save your dad, yes, but not enough to buy the guitar back from the museum."

He considers that for a moment. "Yeah. If I win the first

bet, I guess I'd bet again and hope to get the rest."

"And if you lose the first bet?"

He grimaces. "Then I'll report for duty with Regina tomorrow at noon."

My stomach revolts. I shift my fingers on my steering wheel. "But reporting for duty with Regina tomorrow only earns you twenty-five grand. Would you get your money from Regina and then head straight to the roulette table again?"

I glance over at Aiden. His jaw is clenched. "Honestly, if I lose my first bet and report for duty with Regina, then my new Plan A would become doing literally anything necessary to convince her to pay me the full fifty grand."

Oh, Jesus. I feel like I'm going to vomit.

Aiden continues, "And if that didn't pan out, then, yeah, I guess I'd have no choice at that point but to gamble *Regina's* twenty-five grand and hope to God the roulette wheel comes up black for me on my second try." He rubs his forehead, clearly feeling anxious. "Fuck."

I suddenly feel like I'm going to lose my breakfast. "Aiden, this is horrible. There's got to be another way to get the money you need than playing roulette."

"Hey, if you've got a better idea, I'm all ears. Robbing a bank isn't an option, obviously. There's not enough time to run a long con or make some kind of legitimate investment with the guitar money. And I sure as hell don't have anything left to fucking sell." He sighs. "Look, I'm not an idiot, okay? I know casinos exist to take gamblers' money fifty-one percent of the time. *I know that.* But, still, on any given day, it's possible for a guy to walk into a casino, put it all on black, and walk away a winner. It's possible, Savvy. And I just keep hoping that, maybe, just maybe, today is my lucky day."

My mind is racing. I suddenly feel like there's an elephant sitting on my chest.

"Do you have a better idea than gambling with the twenty-five grand?" he asks.

"No," I admit. "But if you're going to gamble, then you need to gamble smart. Putting everything on black in roulette can't possibly be your best bet in the casino. That would give you only about a forty-seven percent chance of winning—a *fifty-three* percent chance of losing it all in the blink of an eye. I've got to think there's a game with better odds than that."

Aiden rakes his hand through his hair. "I'm all ears. I have no idea what I'm doing. I never gamble."

I glance away from the road to look at Aiden, and the tortured expression on his face breaks my heart. *Shit.* He's right to be nervous. Gambling is ultimately a losing proposition, any way you slice it. Anyone who grew up in Vegas will tell you that. But what would be the point of telling Aiden that right now? He's right. He's got no other practical option than to gamble the money in his backpack and hope today is his lucky day.

"I don't even like to gamble," Aiden mutters, his gaze trained on the highway stretching before us. "My grandfather's two mottos in life were 'Nothing comes for free' and 'Slow and steady wins the race.' He despised get-rich-quick schemes every bit as much as my dad has always chased them." He looks at me. "I know as a teenager I got mixed up in some really stupid shit with my father. I thought his fast life seemed glamorous and exciting compared to the slow and steady life I lived with Gramps. But I'm back to basics now. I work my ass off every day, slow and steady, trying to be the man I was raised to be. But normal rules don't apply right now, Savvy. Not when my father's life hangs in the balance. If those fuckers put a bullet in my dad's head, it'll be even worse for me than losing Mom and Gramps because it'll be my fucking fault."

I look at Aiden in the passenger seat. The poor guy looks like a man on the verge of a nervous breakdown.

"Oh, Aiden," I whisper. "I'm so sorry you're in this position." But that's all I can muster. Nothing in my life has prepared me to handle a situation like this. I truly don't know what to say or do.

We drive in silence for a while. Indeed, we're both quiet for so long, we're still not talking by the time I've exited the freeway and turned my car onto Las Vegas Boulevard.

"I tell you what," I say, my stomach churning. "Let me crunch some numbers, okay? There's got to be a game with better odds than roulette. When we get to the hotel, I'll do some research and figure out a bet that will give you as close to fifty-fifty odds as possible. I don't know what to advise you off the top of my head—my parents never gambled, so I didn't grow up with it. But gambling is nothing but math and probabilities. Totally in my wheelhouse. Let me do some research and tell you what I recommend you do."

"Thanks, Savvy. I'd really appreciate that."

I let out the biggest exhale of my life. I just implicitly nixed our prior agreement to say goodbye the minute we arrive in Las Vegas, and he didn't push back. "Great," I say, trying not to let the relief I feel permeate my tone. "When we get to the room, why don't you lie down and try to relax while I do my thing? Order some room service on me. Have a couple beers." I glance over at him, my heart pounding. "I'm sure you're feeling incredibly stressed out."

He nods. "Thanks. Yeah, I am."

I nod. If I say something, I'm worried Aiden will figure out the sneaky maneuver I just pulled on him.

"I'm surprised your family doesn't gamble," he says as I pull into the long driveway leading to the Bellagio. "I thought everyone in Vegas gambles."

"Nah, people who actually grew up here typically aren't big gamblers. And that's especially true of a girl who grew up with a father who's the head of a math department."

"Would it be okay for me to sleep with you in your room tonight?" Aiden asks. "I haven't actually booked a room for tonight yet."

My heart leaps and bounds and lurches, but I try to make my voice sound breezy and casual. "Of course. I was assuming you'd stay with me tonight."

"Thanks, Savvy. I didn't want to ask if it would make you think I'm taking advantage of you."

I roll my eyes. "Aiden, we're way past that. I know you're not using me for a freaking hotel room. You're using me for sex."

He smiles.

"Seriously, Aiden. You're in a terrible situation, and I'm helping you out because I care about you. It's as simple as that."

"But you're strapped for cash, too," he says.

"Don't worry about me. I prepaid for my room so long

ago, it feels like a free room now. And, regardless, my situation is irrelevant. Yeah, I lost my job. But so what? I'm twenty-three with no family to support. If need be, I can eat macaroni and cheese for the next three months or move in with my mom and aunt in Phoenix. Compared to what you're dealing with, making my mortgage on a fixer-upper condo in West LA is a first-world problem. All that matters to me now—literally, the only thing—is figuring out how to get the money you need to save your dad's life. And once we do that, the very next thing on the list is helping you get back Betty, too."

CHAPTER THIRTEEN

AIDEN

For the past twenty minutes, I've been lying fully clothed alongside Savvy on top of the fluffy white bed in her hotel room, watching her clack on her keyboard and squint at her screen.

"Do you need glasses?" I ask.

"Huh?"

"You're squinting."

"Oh. No. This is the face I make when I'm thinking really hard."

I grin. God, she's adorable. "Carry on."

Savvy returns to her screen.

I rest my cheek in my palm, my eyes fixed on her beautiful face, and watch her for a few minutes longer. "You got any advice for me yet, Savvy Who Isn't Savvy?" I ask.

"No, not yet, Aiden Who Isn't Patient. Hold your horses, hot stuff."

I chuckle. "Wow. Has Savvy Who Isn't Savvy morphed into Savvy Who Doesn't Pull Any Punches?"

"That's what happens when a girl's give-a-shitter done breaks, sweetheart. She loses the ability to sugarcoat."

I laugh, just as my phone buzzes with an incoming text. I pull it out of my pocket, and my stomach clenches sharply at the name on the screen. *Regina.*

Have you made it to LV yet?

I glance up at Savvy, my stomach tight, and find her still engrossed in her laptop. Quickly, I tap out a reply.

No. My motorcycle broke down along the way. Had to arrange some alternative transportation near Barstow. On my way now.

Where are you?

Still in Barstow.

But you're still coming, right?

I grimace. The thought of showing up at Regina's hotel room tomorrow makes me feel physically ill. But, obviously, I've got to keep her on the line.

Yeah. I'll be there.

Regina replies immediately.

Woohoo! This is going to be the best birthday

ever! I got a suite at the Four Seasons for us.
I'm there now and it's spectacular. Be here
tomorrow at noon sharp. You and I are going
to kick off my birthday weekend with a bang.

She tacks her room number to the end of her text, followed by a "blowing kisses" emoji.

I toss my phone onto the mattress without replying, bile rising in my throat. *Fuck.* Maybe the conventional wisdom is that a sixteen-year-old dude should feel flattered or maybe even titillated upon discovering his father's wealthy fuck buddy secretly wants to fuck him, especially when the woman is objectively not terrible looking. But discovering Regina's lusty intentions toward me back in the day never once thrilled me—the discovery only disgusted me from day one. Two years before my first encounter with Regina, I'd come to LA a motherless, grandfatherless teenager in the depths of loneliness and despair. There's never been a kid with a bigger hole in his heart, a more aimless, rudderless child, than I was back then. And that hideous woman's instinct upon meeting me for the first time wasn't to nurture or protect me, but to *fuck* me? And my disgust for Regina only intensified from there, once I started having sex with girls my own age and realized exactly what sex meant. The impact it had on my emotions and soul. The fact that I didn't like to give it away like most guys my age—that I liked it best when it was special.

Of course, I've never told my dad the truth about Regina or the shit she used to constantly imply to me with verbal hints and body language. What if my father actually cared about Regina? I didn't think he did, but I wasn't positive. And

I didn't want to hurt his feelings by telling him the truth. Plus, I didn't want to buy myself a one-way ticket out of my new home if he picked her over me. So I kept my mouth shut. I saw Regina infrequently, after all. Only if I happened to be around when she came by, which she didn't do often, anyway. And, probably, if I'm being honest, I didn't tell my father or anyone the things Regina used to say to me because I was just flat-out embarrassed by them. I thought maybe I'd done something to provoke her—and I didn't know how to explain to the world why a young dude who's supposed to want to fuck anything that moves had absolutely no intention of doing that. And now, here I am. With Savvy. The only person I've ever told about Regina in my life. And I'm awfully glad I never said a word to my father or anyone else, because as it turns out, Regina is quite possibly the only person standing between my father and a bullet to his head.

"Okay, I've figured it out," Savvy says, pulling me out of my dark thoughts. She flashes me an adorable smile that melts me, as usual.

"I'm all ears," I say.

Savvy takes a deep breath. "Just like I thought, putting all your money on black isn't the way to go. Your best bet is craps. Putting the entire twenty-five grand on the pass line in one bet."

"Will that give me a fifty-fifty chance?"

"No, not quite. But close. A hell of a lot closer than roulette. When all statistical possibilities are integrated, your chances of winning at craps are about forty-nine percent. For the first roll, that is. Of course, if you win on the first roll, you'll need to bet twenty-five grand *again* to wind up with the full seventy-five. And if you lose that second bet, then you'll be back where you started with twenty-five grand. Which you could bet again. And if you do that—if you keep trying until you either go broke or make it all the way to seventy-five grand—then my math says you'll have close to a one in three chance of turning your twenty-five thousand into seventy-five. The actual probability is thirty-two point four percent—not quite thirty-three point three—of you walking away with seventy-five grand at the end of today."

"Shit," I whisper, my stomach churning. "There's *less* than a one in three chance of me walking away with the full seventy-five grand?"

She grimaces sympathetically. "Yes."

I let that stomach-churning idea settle in for a long minute. "I knew my chances were bad, but I didn't realize they were *that* bad," I say softly.

Savvy grabs my hand. "You do have some other options besides a pass line bet at craps. At least from a purely mathematical standpoint. There are other games that also yield just under a fifty-fifty chance on a single bet. But I think a pass line bet at craps is the best choice under the totality of circumstances. For one thing, you can bet the full twenty-five grand in a single bet at a high-stakes craps table. Other games probably won't allow a single bet that big. And, full disclosure, there are mathematically better strategies at the craps table than putting the entire sum on the pass line. For instance, you could put part of it on the pass line and make additional bets that 'take the odds.'"

"What's that?"

She explains it to me, and my head feels like it's going to explode.

Savvy adds, "But the potential benefit of employing that strategy is small, and the casino might not allow it at the level of money you'll need to bet. So bottom line, taking all factors into account, my recommendation is a pass line bet at craps."

"Then that's what I'll do. I trust you completely."

She squeezes my hand. "I'm sorry I couldn't figure out something more ironclad for you. Something totally outside the box, maybe. If we'd only had more time, I think I could have come up with *something*. Maybe a high-yield investment for the twenty-five grand? Some product we could buy cheap and sell high? I don't know. I could have called a friend from the finance division of my old job."

Now it's my turn to squeeze Savvy's hand. "It's okay, baby. You've helped me a ton. You've just now increased my odds of winning by a couple percentage points. Who knows? That margin might turn out to be the difference between success and failure for me today."

Her brow knits with deep concern. "I just wish I could do more for you."

I take her face in my hands. "You've already done more for me than you know, Savannah Valentine. You've made me feel hopeful in the midst of the worst shitstorm of my life." I kiss her gently. "*Thank you.*"

She smiles ruefully. "I can't stand the thought of you reporting for duty tomorrow, Aiden. The thought breaks my heart."

I push a lock of dark hair off her forehead and sigh. Shit, shit, shit. I'd love to be able to tell Savvy not to worry—that there's no way in hell I'm actually going to show up at Regina's hotel room tomorrow. That meeting Savvy took that option off the table. But I can't say that and mean it. If I wind up losing all my money at the craps table downstairs in a few minutes— if I'm suddenly penniless *and* guitarless, and I've got no other prospects to save my father's life than fucking Regina, then, by God, I'm going to fuck Regina.

"I'm sorry, Savvy. I couldn't have met you at a worse time in my life."

She nods.

I drop my hands from her beautiful face. "Let's head down to the casino now," I say softly. "I just want to get this shitshow over with, one way or another. I feel sick to my stomach right now."

Savvy looks like she wants to cry, but she puts on her game face. "Let's do it."

I put my finger underneath her chin and gaze into her big, brown eyes. "Hey," I say softly. "No matter what happens down there, chicken girl, I want you to know you're the most incredible girl I've ever met in my life, and I'll never, ever forget you."

CHAPTER FOURTEEN

SAVANNAH

As Aiden and I follow the floor supervisor toward the high-stakes craps table at the far end of the casino, I glance down at the five cranberry-colored casino chips in Aiden's hands. The five cranberry chips he's going to put on the pass line when we reach the craps table—the chips that stand between life and death for Aiden's father.

Aiden's hands are surprisingly steady holding those damned chips, I notice. The man definitely has his nerves in check, unlike me. It's not even my father's life at stake, and I'm shaking like a leaf as we walk. What if Aiden puts those five chips on the pass line and rolls a two, three, or twelve? Just like that, Aiden will have no money and no means of getting any besides reporting for duty with the birthday girl tomorrow and trying his best to "convince" her through "any means necessary" to give him fifty grand instead of twenty-five. Good lord, I don't even want to think about what kind of "convincing" Aiden would be willing to do.

I swallow hard, feeling like I'm walking to my own execution. If Aiden loses all his money on one roll of the dice, will he subliminally blame *me*? I'm the one who advised him to play craps instead of roulette, after all. I realize it wouldn't be rational for Aiden to blame me if he loses all the guitar money in one roll, but gambling isn't a rational enterprise. That's why people "follow their gut" when they gamble. They carry lucky charms. If Aiden loses all his chips in craps, I think a part of him will think, *Shit! I should have followed my gut and bet it all on black!* And even if he doesn't blame me for his loss, I think Aiden is right; it would mark the death knell of our budding romance, regardless. He'd go to Regina, and I'd feel disgusted and jealous and rejected. And that would be it for us. Yes, I'd understand intellectually why Aiden went to Regina. But I wouldn't be able to explain it to my heart. And even if I *could* get over Aiden sleeping with Regina for two solid days while I hung out feeling sorry for myself—even if I could somehow move on from that—I'm sure Aiden would feel so disgusted with himself afterward, the last person in the world he'd want to be with would be the one person in the world who knows his shameful secret. Looking into my face would constantly remind him of what he did.

"Here we are," the floor manager says, indicating the high-rollers craps table before us. It's a table at which peasants like Aiden and me normally wouldn't be allowed to gamble. But Aiden finagled it for us a few minutes ago when he showed the floor manager his five cranberry chips and told him he wanted to put it all on the pass line in one bet. "Stay here, please," the floor manager says, before leaving us to approach the dealer.

Aiden and I exchange a nervous glance and then return our attention to the floor manager chatting with the dealer. The dealer nods. The floor manager gestures to Aiden, signaling he's cleared to play.

Our hands clasped, Aiden and I make our way to the edge of the table and stand stiffly together as we await the end of the current roller's turn.

"You okay?" I whisper.

He doesn't reply for a long beat. "I can't do it," he finally whispers. "I need you to place the bet for me, Savvy." He shoves his chips at me. "Please."

"What?" I push on Aiden's hand. "Not *me*. I'd barf all over the table."

"I need you to roll the dice. I need lady luck. And you have to have chips on the table to be the roller."

I feel like I'm going to tip over. "Aiden, no."

"Please," he whispers. "You're my good luck charm. If I roll and crap out, I'll never forgive myself."

"And if *I* roll and crap out, you'll never forgive *me*."

"Not true," he says, shoving the chips toward me again. "Please, Savvy."

I look into his ocean-blue eyes for a moment. "We'll do it together. I'll roll, but we're *both* going to bet. Three for you and two for me."

"Great. Just as long as you roll, I'm happy. You're way, *way* luckier than me."

That last statement is patently ridiculous. I'm not even slightly lucky. But there's no time to argue with him because the dealer just called out for a new roller.

I signal to the dealer that I'll be rolling and he pushes the dice across the felt table to me.

"We've got a lady roller," the dealer calls out. "Place your bets."

As the well-heeled high rollers at the table place their bets, Aiden and I split up the five cranberry chips between us and then place our respective bets on the pass line.

Aiden smiles tightly at me. "Good luck," he whispers. "And thank you."

I pick up the dice with a shaking hand, feeling like I'm going to hurl.

"You've got this," Aiden whispers.

"Aiden, are you sure you want *me* to—"

"I'm sure," he says. "Don't think about it, chicken girl. Just roll."

Without further ado, I say a prayer, kiss the dice, and toss them toward the far end of the table...and then watch as they bounce across the felt...and hit the bumper on the far end of the table...and then bounce back...and, finally, come to a rest.

A five and six.

The gamblers crowded around the table cheer.

"Eleven!" the dealer calls out. "*Winner!*"

I throw myself into Aiden's waiting arms, and he crushes me in a jubilant hug that knocks the air out of my lungs. The dealer calls out to us to collect our winnings, and we break apart and gleefully collect the five new cranberry chips sitting in front of us on the pass line.

"Holy shit," Aiden says, looking down with wide eyes at the five new and five old chips in his hands. "You did it, Savvy! Oh, my God."

"Place your bets!" the dealer calls out—and Aiden lurches away from the table like it's on fire.

The players at the table begin a new round while Aiden

stands ten feet away, staring at his ten chips with bug eyes.

I stand next to him, my heart racing, too freaked out to ask him what he's going to do next.

"This is my dad's life right here," Aiden says softly, staring at his hands. "These chips are *literally* the only thing standing in the way of my dad getting a bullet to his head." He lets out a shaky exhale and looks at me. "I thought I'd have the balls to make another bet. But now that I'm here, and I know I've got my dad's life saved for sure, I can't risk it."

My stomach flips over. Does he mean he's decided to forfeit the opportunity to buy back his grandfather's guitar...or that he's intending to report for duty with Regina tomorrow?

Aiden chews on the inside of his cheek for a long moment, apparently lost in thought. "What would you do in my shoes, Savvy? Tell me the truth. Would you bet again or stop?"

Shit. As much as I want Aiden to try to parlay the fifty grand in his hand into seventy-five, there's no doubt what I'd do. No doubt what *he* should do. "I wouldn't risk it," I reply honestly. "Nothing matters more than saving your father's life. Now that you've done that, you should stop."

Aiden closes his eyes and nods.

There's a long moment of nausea-inducing silence. "So now what?" I finally whisper. I clutch my chest, bracing myself for his answer.

"I don't know," Aiden says. "I've got to think about it. At the end of the day, which will be worse? Living without Betty for the rest of my life or spending two days in hell?"

Oh, dear God. Aiden is seriously considering being that woman's boy toy for two solid days? "Let's gamble some more and try to win the twenty-five grand you need," I blurt. "Not with that fifty-grand. We won't touch those ten chips, no matter what. We'll gamble with..." I look down at my hand, my heart thumping. "With my ring!" I blurt. "I'll hawk it and gamble with the money!"

"No, Savvy."

"Yes!" My heart is racing. I feel desperate. Panicky. "My ring is worth about three grand, I think. Yes, it'll be a tall order to turn three grand into twenty-five. But it's worth a try."

"*No*," Aiden says sharply. "Your father gave you that ring. You told me it's your most-prized possession."

"I don't care about the ring. In fact, it'll be better for my mental health to use it to help you than to wear it and be constantly reminded my father doesn't love me anymore."

Aiden looks pained. "Aw, Savvy." He touches my shoulder. "Your father still loves you. People aren't perfect. They fuck up. That doesn't mean they don't still *love*."

Tears flood my eyes. "I don't want to talk about my father. I shouldn't have brought him up. All that matters is I want to help you. Please, Aiden. Let me help you." I grab his arm. "I want to see what might happen between us back in LA. And if you have sex with that woman for two days, we both know that won't be possible. What we're feeling will get tainted by my irrational jealousy and your self-loathing and we'll be over before we started."

He looks emotional, but he shakes his head. "I can't let you hawk that ring. It's your Betty. If you lose it trying to help me, you'll never forgive me. And then we'd be dead in the water, regardless."

I wipe my eyes. "I admit I love this ring. But I'd sell it in a heartbeat to help you. Especially if helping you would mean I'd get to see you again after today."

Aiden presses his lips together for a moment. "Thank you," he says softly. "But you'd be hawking it in vain. We both know I'd lose every dime of the ring money long before we came close to winning twenty-five grand. And then I'd be in the same situation I'm in right now. Sitting on fifty grand from craps and needing twenty-five grand more. The only difference would be you'd be out of a ring, and I'd feel like shit about it."

My lower lip is trembling. I swallow hard to keep myself from losing it. "I'm not ready to say goodbye to you. I've never felt this kind of electricity with someone. I'm greedy. I don't want it to end."

"Aw, Savvy. *Baby.*" He stuffs his cranberry chips into his jeans and puts his hands on my cheeks. "I'm so sorry I dragged you into this. Every fiber of my being told me to leave you out of it, but I just couldn't resist you. I was selfish. I'm so sorry."

"Don't be sorry. I'm glad you couldn't resist me."

"I'm no good for you," he whispers. "Can't you see that? You're way out of my league. You should walk away."

"Stop saying stuff like that. Just stop. I don't care about your résumé, Aiden. All I care about is how you make me *feel.* And I can honestly say you make me feel like nobody ever has."

He wraps his arms around me and squeezes me tightly, and I melt into him and let my tears flow. Losing my dad six months ago. Losing my job yesterday. Being humiliated by Derek yesterday, not to mention Mason Crenshaw five years before that. It's all been too much to take. I don't want to lose

Aiden, too. I'm fully aware I don't know him yet. For all I know, these feelings I'm having for Aiden might be nothing more than a projection. A fantasy. A beautiful dream. But I don't care. I want this beautiful dream to keep going. I want to find out if this dream could possibly become a reality.

"Let's get out of here," Aiden says softly into my ear. "I need to think about my decision, and I can't do it here with all the noise and lights. I need quiet. I need to make music."

I pull back and look at him quizzically.

He wipes the tears from my cheekbone with the pad of his thumb. "Let's find a piano somewhere, chicken girl. There's a song I haven't been able to get out of my head since the taco place. I'm dying to play it for you."

CHAPTER FIFTEEN

SAVANNAH

Holy crap.

Aiden MacAllister is a musical genius.

I figured he'd be a skilled musician. I figured he'd inherited at least some of his mother's and grandfather's talent, either through DNA or simple osmosis. I also figured a popular restaurant in Silver Lake wouldn't pay Aiden to perform every Sunday if he wasn't pretty good. LA has its pick of talented troubadours, after all. And Aiden said the tips he earns at his Sunday gigs are his biggest source of income each week. So, yes, I expected Aiden MacAllister to be pretty talented. *But not this talented.*

For the past few minutes, Aiden's been playing piano and singing to me in a storage room at the Bellagio—a room the catering manager led us to when Aiden flashed her his most charming smile and asked if there was "a spare piano somewhere in this big ol' hotel" he might play for a bit, "just to unwind." And I've been rendered speechless since the moment he started tickling the ivories.

But it's not Aiden's piano playing that's astounding me; it's his voice. *Oh, God, Aiden's voice.* It's mesmerizing. Swoon-worthy. Soulful. Honest. And this song he's serenading me with? It's perfection. It's not his song, actually. It's John Mayer's. "Daughters." But Aiden is making the song his own as he sings. And, holy hell, he's giving me all the feels. After everything that's happened in my life recently, I feel like this song was written specifically for me.

When Aiden finishes singing, I blink back the tears welling in my eyes. "Beautiful," I whisper. "You're amazing."

Aiden grins. "Thanks. I've had that song running through my head on a loop since you told me about your dad at the taco place. It feels so good to finally get to play it for you."

I wipe my eyes. "I loved it. Will you play me another one? Maybe a song of yours?"

"Absolutely. But first..." Aiden pushes my dark hair behind my shoulder and lays a soft kiss on the bare nape of my neck. He trails soft kisses up my neck...to my jaw...and, finally, presses his lips against mine. I slide my palm onto his cheek and kiss him passionately, with every emotion I'm feeling in this moment. Excitement. Heartache. Joy. Arousal. *Yearning.* And Aiden returns my kiss with equal fervor. Indeed, his kiss feels so full of emotion, it's taking my breath away. When we finally pull apart, I feel like I'm going to tip over.

"What was that for?" I whisper, my heart racing.

"For the way you were looking at me while I was singing." I blush.

He lays a soft kiss on my cheek. "Okay, chicken girl. I'm gonna play you my favorite song of all the ones I've written. And, trust me, I've written a lot." He lays his beautiful hands on the keys of the piano and begins singing me a song—a song

I'd guess, judging by the lyrics, was inspired by his grandfather and mother. It's a song about love and loss. But, mostly, loss. A song about taking solace in happy memories. About finding light in the dark. Oh, God, this song is breaking my freaking heart.

My phone vibrates on top of the piano with an incoming call. It's Derek's name on my screen.

Aiden's eyes drift to my phone. He abruptly stops playing. "Is that the douchebag?"

I nod.

"Answer it."

"What would be the point?"

"You deserve to hear him grovel. Let him grovel for a bit and then tell him to fuck off."

I shrug and press a button to answer the call on speaker phone. "Hi, Derek."

"Jesus Christ, Savvy!" Derek roars. "You didn't give me a chance to explain! I never said we were exclusive! If that's what you *assumed*, then I can't be expected to—"

I disconnect the call. "I guess he didn't call to grovel."

Aiden clenches his jaw. "Douchebag."

The phone rings with another incoming call. Derek again.

"May I?" Aiden says.

"Sure."

Aiden answers the call on speaker phone. "Hello, Derek."

"Who the fuck is this?" Derek barks.

"The guy who's been lucky enough to be with Savvy since you cheated on her."

"Is this the asshole from the videos—the guy with the

stupid guitar tattoo on his forearm?"

"The one and only," Aiden says.

"Fuck you, you piece of shit!" Derek roars. He lets out a growl that can only be described as primal. "I can't imagine how drunk you had to get Savvy to get her to fuck you on Wednesday—mere hours after meeting you. Let alone to agree to let you videotape her, too! What'd you do, asshole? Did you roofie her, you piece of shit? Because the Savvy Valentine I know would *never* agree to—"

I lean into the phone. "*Wrong.* Savvy Valentine *would* and Savvy Valentine *did.* Willingly, consensually, and quite happily." I wink at Aiden, and he flashes me a stunning smile. "The truth is I've left my corporate job to become a porn star, Derek."

Aiden chuckles. "That's right, baby! We're the porn star and the felon!"

"What? Savvy, is this guy seriously a *felon*?"

"He is. As it turns out, felons are extra hot in bed. All that pent-up frustration while they were sitting in a prison cell, I guess."

Aiden and I share a huge laugh.

"Savvy, talk to me," Derek says, his tone turning decidedly concerned. "Is this guy holding you against your will? Are you drugged right now?"

"No, Derek. I'm perfectly sober. My give-a-shitter done broke, that's all."

"You're...what?"

Aiden leans into my phone. "*Her give-a-shitter done broke.*"

"Hey, asshole!" Derek yells. "Shut the fuck up, okay? I wasn't talking to you. I was talking to Savvy."

"Fuck you," Aiden roars. "Savvy's done talking to you, you piece of shit."

"Oh, *I'm* the piece of shit?" Derek roars back. "You think it's okay to lure sweet, innocent young women into making nasty sex videos with you, motherfucker?"

Aiden rises from the piano bench, suddenly enraged. "Hey, *asshole*," he shouts toward my phone, a vein in his neck throbbing. "You want to talk about a guy luring sweet, innocent young women, then let's talk about *you*. How many women have you lured to the top of that mountain, asshole? How many times have you told a girl you love her, just to get your dick wet, huh? You better pray you never go to prison, fuckwad, or the guys in there would sniff your pussy-ass out in a heartbeat and make mincemeat out of you."

Derek growls like a grizzly bear. "Is that so? Well, you'd better hope and pray I never find you, motherfucker, because the minute I see that stupid fucking guitar tattoo, I'm gonna know—"

Aiden disconnects the call. He sits back down and takes a deep, steadying breath. "You actually *liked* that tool?"

"I believe I mentioned I was more flattered by Derek's attention than anything."

Aiden rolls his eyes. "He's an idiot."

"Thanks for jumping in to defend me. You're my knight in shining armor, Aiden MacAllister."

"Anytime, my pretty little chicken princess."

I bat my eyelashes and motion to the piano. "Now, where

were we? I believe you were playing me a song."

"Yeah." He shakes out his arms and exhales. "*Fuckwad.*"

"Forget him. He doesn't matter. Play me a song."

Aiden takes another deep breath and his shoulders visibly relax. "Okay. I'll play you another song I wrote." He plays me a new song, and I swoon and sigh throughout. Finally, he finishes, and I clap and kiss him.

"I suck on piano," Aiden says. "But you get the gist."

"You don't suck on piano. You're amazing."

"I'm way more comfortable on guitar. That's my main instrument."

"Wow. You're better on guitar? Damn. Then you must be out of this world. Honestly, Aiden, with that voice of yours and all that charisma and good looks, I can't fathom why you're not a huge star."

"Thanks." He shrugs. "The music biz is a tough nut to crack. Tough for anyone, but especially an ex-con. But it's okay. I've long since stopped dreaming of becoming a rock star playing arenas. All I dream about now is making a simple living from music. If I could get steady session work and a few high-paying, live gigs a month, I'd be thrilled."

"Hey, don't people sometimes get discovered on YouTube? You could post some clips of yourself there."

"Oh, I already have. And so have my fans."

"You've got fans?"

"It's all relative. But, yeah. There are a bunch of people who follow me around from gig to gig. Show up on Sundays pretty regularly. They've actually posted a ridiculous amount of videos of me. But so far, that hasn't gotten me anywhere."

He winks. "It's cool. I'm happy just playing, whether it's a restaurant patio or a club."

I grab my phone. "Where are the videos? I didn't see a single one when I ran that background check on you."

"Oh. Yeah. I don't use my real name when I perform. All my music stuff is under the name Aiden Jameson. Jameson is my dad's last name."

"Oh, I love it." I quickly run the search, and, lo and behold, Aiden Jameson is all over the damned place, mostly thanks to videos uploaded by audience members at his various gigs. I click on one video, and there's Aiden playing an electric guitar with a band in what appears to be a small club.

"Is that Betty?" I ask, indicating Aiden's guitar in the video.

"No. That's my Strat. Betty's a Tele. A Fender Telecaster. I only bring Betty out for special gigs. I'll show you." I give him my phone, and he navigates to a video. "*That's* my baby."

Onscreen, Aiden is playing an electric guitar in a band full of old guys. They're on a small stage in a dimly lit club, and every man in the band, including Aiden, looks like he's having the time of his life. "Those are all my grandfather's best friends from back in the day," Aiden says. "I went to Nashville for a bit after I first got out of prison. I visited Gramps's grave and told him I was sorry for screwing up so badly. I promised him it'd never happen again. And then I wound up jamming with those guys at the club where Gramps used to jam every Thursday night. It was one of the best nights of my life."

I watch the video for a long moment, and my heart swells...and then aches. The joy Aiden is feeling on that stage is palpable. It breaks my heart to think he might never get to experience that specific brand of joy again.

When the video ends, I set my phone back onto the piano, resolve washing over me. "That's it. I'm going to hawk my ring, and we're going to gamble with the proceeds and do our best to win twenty-five grand. We might not succeed—in fact, the odds are against us. But at least we'll know we tried. No regrets."

"No *regrets*?" Aiden says incredulously. He shakes his head. "Savvy, I'd have a mountain of regrets if you lost your most-prized possession because of me."

"But what if we win?" I say. "Aiden, I can make sure we gamble *smart*. I'm a whiz with numbers. I could count cards in Blackjack or something."

"Count cards?" He scoffs. "The dealer or floor manager would figure you out in a heartbeat and kick us the fuck out. Or they'd figure you out and change the rules. Mid-hand, if necessary. Successfully counting cards in a casino is a great plotline in a movie, but in real life, it rarely works. Casinos are *really* good at spotting it, baby."

"I could read up on it," I insist. "I'm much smarter than I look."

His features melt with affection. "I know you're smart, honey. But I'm telling you it wouldn't work."

I sigh. "Poker, then?"

"Have you ever played poker before?"

"Yes. A couple times."

"In a casino with professional card players?"

My shoulders droop. "No. In college. In the dorm with friends. But I could read up on it and learn. I'm a quick learner.

You'd be shocked how fast I pick stuff up."

Aiden shakes his head. "Thanks for wanting to help me so badly, baby, but we don't have time for you to read up and learn. And even if we did, poker isn't only about the cards in your hand. It's about reading people. Being able to bluff. You need street smarts, sweetheart. And, let's face it, that's not your strong suit."

My stomach falls into my toes. Truer words were never spoken. "Okay, then. How about craps?"

Aiden takes my hand and looks at me ruefully. "Stop, Savvy. Please. Any game we pick, we'd have to win over and over again to grow our seed money all the way to twenty-five grand. And we both know the odds of that happening are miniscule. I got lucky once today, at exactly the right time. I'm not stupid enough to think I'd do it again and again and again."

I hang my head. He's right. I know he is. But that doesn't stop me from wanting to try every damned thing I can to help him.

"Savvy, that ring means the world to you," Aiden says softly. "It was written all over your face when you told me about it."

"I'm willing to risk it," I say softly.

"Hey."

I lift my face and look into his ocean-blue eyes.

"Tell me the truth," he says. "What are our chances of turning three grand into twenty-five? Do the math."

I chew the inside of my cheek and crunch the numbers in my head. "Eleven point five percent," I finally say. "A little better than one chance in nine we'd hit our goal."

"That's about what I figured. And that's assuming you could get three grand for the ring, right? For all we know, your valuation is optimistic."

I press my lips together. He's right, actually. I was definitely being optimistic when I said I could get three grand for the ring. I hang my head with resignation. "I just want to help you so much."

"I know that. Thank you. But some things can't be helped. Trust me, if anyone knows that life lesson, it's me." He touches my cheek and smiles. "Thank you, sweetheart. As my Gramps used to say, 'you're a peach.' But some things just suck, and there's nothing you can do about it. It's okay. That's life."

Looking into his beautiful face, I have the sudden, overpowering urge to ask him what he's decided about tomorrow. Has he decided he can live with two days of hell to get his beloved guitar back? But I'm too big a coward to ask him that question directly, so I skirt around the issue. "Were you able to do some thinking while paying piano?"

"Not really," he says. "Hard to think when there's a pretty girl looking at you like you're Prince Charming."

I blush.

"I think it's the kind of thing I've got to *not* think about for a while for my mind to figure out what to do."

I nod slowly, too overwhelmed to speak. *He's still considering reporting for duty as that woman's boy toy tomorrow?*

Aiden moves my hair behind my shoulder and sighs. "Honestly, I don't want to think about all that stuff for a while. I almost stroked out during that craps game. I need a break."

He smiles ruefully. "All I want to do tonight is hang out with my beautiful chicken princess and forget everything. Now that I've got the money to save my dad, I want to forget the world and take you on a date. A real date. Let's walk along the Strip. Check out the fountain. Do some people watching. Grab dinner." He kisses the top of my hand. "And then I'll take you back to our room and get you naked and fuck the living hell out of you and get to feel that crazy electricity one more blessed time before reality comes crashing in."

CHAPTER SIXTEEN

AIDEN

I kiss every inch of Savvy's body, not knowing if I'll get the chance to do it ever again. Every inch. Her milky thighs. The curve of her hips. Her belly button. Her rib cage. The delicate flesh between her legs. *And I savor her.* I suck on her breast and then take her hard nipple into my mouth. I swirl my tongue over the hard bud and nibble her until she's moaning. I work my way to her neck and bite and suck until she's swollen and red—marked as mine. At least for tonight. *Mine.*

I work my way back down Savvy's body to her pussy again. This time to stay awhile. I slide my fingers inside her heat and lap at her swollen, hard clit with a voracious tongue. And there I stay, reveling in her. Consuming her. *Owning her.* When Savvy comes against my fingers and tongue, she grits out my name...and every fiber of me surges at the delicious sound. I turn her over on the bed and guide her to her hands and knees and plunge myself inside her from behind. Playtime is over. I want her to understand she's mine now. That she'll never get fucked so well again, as long as she lives.

I grab Savvy's dark hair as I fuck her hard. With all my might, in fact. I want nothing more than to give this girl a fuck she'll never forget. I yank firmly on Savvy's hair, pulling her head back, lean over her back, and whisper into her ear, "Nobody will ever fuck you like this again. No matter what happens, a little piece of you will always be mine."

She makes a garbled sound and then spits out, "*Yes.*"

And that simple word turns me the fuck on. So I fuck her harder. And grope her breast with my free hand as I do it.

We're growling like wild animals now.

She's saying my name, over and over again, with each thrust of my body into hers.

And I'm saying hers.

My breathing is labored.

My entire body is trembling.

I'm dripping in sweat.

Teetering on the edge of pure ecstasy.

Savvy's body stiffens. And then those incredible convulsions around my cock start. And then my balls are treated to a little trickle of warm wetness. *And I'm gone.* Coming so hard, I'm seeing stars. I grip her hair hard as I come. Moan her name. The pleasure is knocking the air out of my lungs. Frying my brain. Making me want to forget my problems and stay with her inside this little fuck-bubble forever.

We crumple onto the mattress, both of us gasping for air. And suddenly, just that fast, I remember the dark cloud hanging over me. Will those asshats stay true to their word and release my father unharmed when I bring them the fifty grand? Or will they take the money and kill us both on the spot?

I press myself into Savvy's sweaty back and stroke her hair. "Savvy," I whisper softly. But that's all I can muster.

Could I possibly turn my back on Betty tomorrow—on my grandfather's *legacy*—to take a shot with a girl I only just met? And will I even get the chance to make that choice, or will I wind up dying an inglorious death tomorrow while trying to buy back my father's life in a motel room in Henderson?

"Aiden," Savvy whispers. She takes my hand and kisses it gently. "If this truly is it for us, I want you to know I'll never forget you."

Oh, my heart. Why couldn't I have met this girl next week when this horrible situation was over? Sighing, I pull Savvy closer to me and clutch her tightly to me from behind. "Savvy, you're a beautiful dream," I say. And then, because I have too many anxious thoughts racing in my head, all at once, I close my eyes and will myself to drift off to sleep.

CHAPTER SEVENTEEN

SAVANNAH

Friday, 8:22 a.m.

I wake up to find Aiden dressed and showered and walking quietly toward the door of our room, his backpack slung over his shoulder, his body language tight. My heart lurches into my throat. Last night's "date" was amazing from start to finish. It was *electric*. And now it seems Aiden is tiptoeing away, possibly for good, without bothering to say goodbye to me.

"Aiden," I say, stopping him dead in his tracks.

He turns, his face flushed. "I didn't want to wake you," he says softly. He motions to a small table on the far side of the room. "I left a note."

I glance over to where he's indicating and, sure enough, there's a small square of paper sitting on the table. "What time is it?" I ask, blood whooshing into my ears.

"Almost eight thirty."

My stomach clenches. Did the birthday girl offer Aiden a bonus to show up for his "job" a few hours early? "Where are you going?" I ask, and then I hold my breath, bracing for his reply.

"To free my father," he says. "The motel where they're

holding him is about twenty minutes away. I've got the fifty-grand right here." He indicates his backpack.

"Is it safe for you to go alone? Aren't the men holding your father dangerous?"

"I'll be fine. They've got no beef with me. They just want their money." But he doesn't look so sure.

"How are you getting there?"

"There's a line of taxis at the front of the hotel."

"Take my car," I say. I gesture toward my purse on a dresser. "The keys are in my purse."

Aiden looks like he feels sick. "It's okay. I don't want to put you out."

Holy hell. He's planning to head straight to the birthday girl's hotel after paying his father's debt, isn't he? I can feel it in my bones. Either that, or he's leaving himself the option. "I insist," I say, my eyes locked onto his. And I'm not just being nice. If Aiden takes my car, then he'll have to come back to return my keys before heading back out, if, indeed that's his plan. Which means, even if he's currently settled on reporting for duty with Regina at noon, I'll have the opportunity to try to convince him face to face not to do it. To try to persuade him to take a leap of faith. To believe we'll get lucky on the casino floor simply because we're meant to be. Yes, I realize the odds are low we'll be able to win twenty-five grand gambling, but it's not *impossible.* Maybe I'll convince him that, even if we were unsuccessful in the casino, that would be okay because we just might turn into something he'd cherish even more than his beloved guitar. Plus, come on! Does Aiden really think getting his guitar back through screwing Regina, a woman he loathes, will make him feel good in the long run? I can't imagine he'll ever feel joy again while playing his guitar if he gets it back like *that*.

"I've really got to go," he says, his voice strained.

"Take the car," I reply, my dark eyes trained on his baby blues. "There's no need for you to spend money on a cab, and I'm not going anywhere today. I'm just going to hang out at the hotel pool."

Aiden looks like he's waging a fierce tug of war inside his head. But after a moment, he nods and says, "Thanks."

My heart leaps. I'll definitely get to see him again! And when I do, God as my witness, I'm going to somehow convince him not to sell himself to Regina. But that's a conversation for another time—for after his father is safe and sound. "My keys are in my purse," I say evenly, gesturing.

"Thanks." Aiden walks to my purse and retrieves my keys. And then he stoically strides to me, bends down, and kisses my forehead. "You're an amazing girl, Savannah Valentine. Best girl I've ever met."

Goose bumps erupt on my arms. Why did that feel like a final goodbye? "Have you decided what to do about Betty?" I blurt, even though I had absolutely no intention of saying it and forcing his hand.

"Honestly, I'm too wound up about my dad to think about that right now. Once I know my dad is out of danger, I'll make a decision on that." He looks at his watch. His face is pale. His features tight. "I better go. Thanks for letting me borrow the car. I really appreciate it."

"Of course."

He pivots to leave.

"Be careful," I say, my heart clanging. "Stay safe."

"Will do." With that, he adjusts his backpack on his shoulder and marches out the door...and, quite possibly, out of my life for good.

When the door clicks behind Aiden, I leap out of bed and scramble to the note he left on the table. And when I see his words, my stomach drops into my toes.

Savvy,

I went to pay my dad's debt. Last night was incredible. I'll never forget it. You're perfect, Savvy. Beautiful. Never let anyone make you doubt your awesomeness ever again.

Much love,

Aiden

CHAPTER EIGHTEEN

AIDEN

Friday, 9:08 a.m.

As I step into the motel room, my heart whacks forcefully against my sternum.

Dad is sitting on one of two saggy beds in the room. A guy in a green track suit is sitting on the other bed, aiming a handgun straight at Dad's head. And a guy in a black leather jacket is sitting in a chair at a small table, smoking a cigarette.

"Aidy," my father whispers. He looks rumpled and exhausted. He's got a black eye. *But he's alive.*

My Adam's apple bobs. "You okay?"

"I'm fine."

"You brought the money?" the guy seated at the table says.

I hold up a white envelope. "Fifty grand."

The guy at the table motions for me to bring him the envelope and, somehow, I command my legs to walk across the room.

I hand the guy the envelope, my traitorous hand visibly shaking.

"Take three steps back," the guy says. "And don't speak."

I do as I'm told.

I watch the guy open the envelope, pull out the entire stack of bills stuffed inside, lay them onto the table next to him, and then slowly, ever so slowly, methodically, torturously begin counting the money.

As the guy counts the bills, I glance at my father. His eyes lock with mine and he winks at me. In reply, I shoot him a look that says, *If we get out of this, I swear to God, I'm gonna beat your fucking ass.*

My heartbeat crashing in my ears, I return to the guy at the table just in time to watch him count the last four bills.

"It's all here," he declares. He smiles at my father the way a shark smiles at a sea lion. "You've got a good son here, Nick. Lucky for you." He takes a long drag of his cigarette and gestures to my father. "Come here."

My dad rises from the bed and walks toward the guy, his jaw tight.

When Dad reaches him, the guy rises from his chair and stands mere inches from him like he's going to kiss him. Or dance with him. Or maybe spit in his face. Slowly, he raises his palm and pats Dad on his cheek. "Next time, Antonio won't be quite so forgiving. You understand me, Nick?"

Dad nods.

The guy gestures toward the door. "You can go."

"It's been fun." Dad turns, grabs my arm with a fierce grip, and yanks me toward the door.

We take one step. Then two. Three. Each step feeling like it's taking an eternity.

I hear movement behind me. Is that the sound of track suit guy raising the gun and aiming it at the back of Dad's head?

At the back of mine?

We make it to the door. Dad reaches for the doorknob and turns it.

And I suddenly realize I can barely breathe.

Dad pushes me through the door and we're out and running down the motel hallway, sprinting at top speed, both of us muttering phrases like "holy fuck!" and "oh my fucking God!" and "run, run, run!" as we go.

We reach Savvy's car and pile inside and I peel out of the parking lot like a man possessed, my knuckles white on the steering wheel and my foot like lead on the gas pedal.

Finally, when we're about two blocks from the motel and my heart has slowed enough for me to breathe again, I turn to my father, shake my head, and say, "Jesus fucking Christ, Dad."

Dad chuckles. "I've never been so happy to see anyone in my goddamned life."

CHAPTER NINETEEN

AIDEN

Friday, 9:48 a.m.

"Thank God Savvy was the one who rolled the dice," I say to my father. I put down my coffee mug. "My hands were shaking so bad, I couldn't roll. I gave the dice to Savvy and closed my eyes, and, two seconds later, I heard everyone at the table cheering. I opened my eyes and there it was: lucky number eleven."

"Amazing," Dad says.

"A fucking miracle."

My father and I are sitting across from each other in a diner about fifteen miles from the Strip. We're celebrating Dad's newfound freedom over breakfast. We've already talked about this morning's harrowing events, and now I'm filling Dad in on how I got the fifty grand.

Dad shoves a forkful of scrambled eggs into his mouth. "I'm sure if you'd have been the one to roll the dice, you'd have rolled an eleven, too. You've always been a lucky bastard."

I gape at my father like he's just shouted, "Someone, please, cut off my penis!"

"Dad, I'm the *unluckiest* bastard I know."

Dad picks up his coffee mug. "Bullshit. You're lucky as hell. Lucky. As. Hell." He flashes me a cocky smile. "You get it from me, actually. I've always been a lucky bastard, too."

Okay, now he's rendered me speechless.

"Well, you've always been *my* lucky charm, anyway," Dad says, apparently reacting to my facial expression. "From the minute you showed up on my doorstep, I couldn't lose."

"Says the guy who just completed a five-year stint in the pen."

Dad scoffs. "That doesn't mean I'm *unlucky*. I did the crime, so I did the time. If I *didn't* do the crime but did the time, anyway, *then* I'd be unlucky. See how that works?" He winks. "Cause and effect, son. It's as simple as that."

I shake my head, but I can't help returning his broad smile. There's no one quite like my father.

"If I'm not lucky as hell, then how do you explain *you*?" Dad continues. "The condom broke *one time* with your mother—one fucking time in *three* months of us screwing like rabbits—and, *boom*, there you were like a four-leaf clover on my doorstep fourteen years later."

I chuckle. If ever I wondered, even for a second, why I sold Betty to that museum to save my father's sorry ass, he just reminded me in spades. "Okay, you've convinced me," I say. "You're the luckiest bastard who ever lived, Dad."

"Second luckiest. *You're* the luckiest."

"Obviously." I raise my coffee mug, chuckling. "To the two luckiest bastards who ever lived."

"Cheers," Dad says. He clinks his mug to mine. But, in a heartbeat, his smile fades and emotion washes over him.

"Seriously, though. Thanks for coming to my rescue, Aidy. If it wasn't for you, I'd have been a goner."

"Yeah, well, it was a one-time thing. Even if I wanted to save your sorry ass again, I'm all out of shit to sell, man."

"Oh, no worries about that. I'm gonna be a saint from now on."

"In all seriousness, Dad. *Please*. Don't fuck up again. I sent those fuckers every dime of my savings. Betty's gone. And my bike broke down on the way here. I *literally* have nothing left to sell to help you again."

Dad looks deeply sorry. "I'm so sorry about all that. The money you sent. Betty. Especially Betty. I know how much you loved that damned guitar."

"You're worth more to me than any guitar. Even Betty."

I clear my throat to keep emotion at bay, grab my fork, and take a big bite of sausage.

"So tell me about this 'amazing' girl you've been hanging out with," Dad says.

"Her full name is actually Savannah, but she goes by Savvy." A huge smile spreads across my face. Just thinking about Savvy instantly brightens my mood. "She's sweet, smart, funny. Sexy as hell. The total package. Honestly, she's the greatest girl I've ever met. She's got book smarts enough to fill the Grand Canyon, but not enough street smarts to plug a ladybug's asshole."

Dad laughs.

"The first time I met her," I continue, "she was like, 'I'm Savvy, but don't let the name fool you.'"

"Talk about an easy mark."

"That's exactly what I thought when she said that! Man, the old me would have had a field day with her. I've been calling her Savvy Who Isn't Savvy."

"And you don't have a twitchy trigger finger at all with her?"

"Nope. Just the opposite. The more she trusts me, the more I want to deserve her trust. Like I keep telling you, Dad. I'm off the con for good. And even if I weren't, meeting Savvy would have reformed me. The only thing I want to do when it comes to Savvy Valentine is protect her from guys like I used to be. Guys like *you*."

"Hey, I'm off the con for good, too, same as you."

"Says the guy who just had to pay fifty grand to avoid getting a bullet to his head."

"That debt was from *before* I went into the joint. I came out a new man, same as you. And even if I hadn't come out straight, I'd be straight now after getting this second chance at life, thanks to you." He leans back in his chair and grins. "Plus, now that I've met Bethany, I can't risk getting locked up again. I've got too much to lose."

"Bethany?" I ask.

"My girlfriend. She's on her way to pick me up."

"She's on her way to Vegas, you mean, or to this diner?"

"The diner. She lives in Vegas. I met her in LA a month ago, right after I got out of the joint, and we both felt like we'd been hit by a thunderbolt. She was visiting her sister in LA and wound up staying way longer than she'd intended, just to hang out with me. But, finally, she had to come back to Vegas last week for a big jewelry convention, so I joined her. That's how I got nabbed by Antonio's goons, actually. I was helping Bethany at her booth at the jewelry convention, and one of his men happened to spot me."

"Really? I assumed you got nabbed at a casino."

"Nope. I haven't stepped foot in a casino since I got out. I told you I'm a new man."

"Sure, Dad. I'll believe it when I see it." I glance at the clock on the wall, and my stomach twists. Ten seventeen. Shit. Time's running out. I've got to decide what to do. What the fuck would Gramps tell me to do about Betty? Would he tell me to stop being a "drama queen" about Regina—that I should bite the bullet and go to her? That it's just two short days of discomfort in exchange for getting to spend the rest of my life playing a guitar that gives me more pleasure than words can express? Or would he tell me nothing, not even Betty, is worth forfeiting my self-respect? And, of course, there's also the twenty-five-thousand-dollar question: Would Gramps's advice change if he knew how I'm feeling about Savvy?

Savvy.

God, I'm so confused. How could I possibly even think about choosing Savvy over Betty when Savvy and I could easily get back to LA and immediately realize we're just too different to make it work? That our whirlwind romance was nothing but a crazy blip fueled by the high-stress circumstances, lust, and booze? I can't imagine it, but it's possible. How would I feel if I were to give up Betty only to get home and have Savvy realize she could never be with a guy like me in real life? Which means, fuck it, I should definitely... What should I do? I still don't know. I close my eyes and try to imagine myself playing

Betty in some club, knowing full well Savvy Valentine was out there in the world, somewhere, feeling rejected and hurt. I imagine myself playing Betty while knowing Savvy was out in the world, fucking some other guy...and my heartrate spikes. And then I torture myself by imagining Savvy not just fucking someone else, but falling in love with him...and I suddenly feel like I'm having a heart attack.

"I wish I would have been able to talk to you again and suggest that to you," Dad says, pulling me out of my thoughts. And, suddenly, I realize Dad's been talking the whole time I've been letting my thoughts run wild.

"What? Sorry."

"I was saying I wish there were some way you could buy your guitar back from that museum. You know, like in a year or something? I wish I would have been able to talk to you again after our conversation on Wednesday to suggest that idea to you. But I didn't think of it when you said you were going to head straight to the museum."

Man, I hate not telling my father about the buyback provision I negotiated with the museum. But I can't. If I tell him about it, he might do something stupid to get me the money, the same way he did something stupid to help Uncle Jimmy. Not to mention, if I tell him about the buyback provision, then I'd probably wind up telling him about Regina's indecent proposal, too. And I don't want to do that. He doesn't need to know I called Regina, begging her to help me save my father's life, and she used my desperation as leverage to make her "Mrs. Robinson" fantasies come true.

"It's okay," I say. "Don't worry about Betty. All that matters is you're okay."

Dad scratches his chin. "But still, even if you didn't negotiate any kind of buyback rights with the museum, do you think they'd let you buy it back anyway if you showed up with twice the money in a year? Because if Bethany and I wind up making a killing with her jewelry business, I'd give you fifty grand to buy it back."

I rub my face. "There's no point in talking about this, Dad."

Dad sighs. "I just feel so guilty you sold Betty for me. I know how much you loved that damned guitar."

"Yeah, well, I love you more."

Dad's face lights up with an epiphany. "Hey, maybe Savvy could loan you some money. It's worth a shot, don't you think? And when Bethany's jewelry business takes off, I'll pay Savvy back with interest."

I roll my eyes. "Savvy doesn't have money, Dad. She's in debt up to her eyeballs, thanks to a condo she bought. And I'd never take money from her, anyway. She already offered to help me try to buy the guitar back and I said no. She offered to hawk a ring of hers worth a couple grand and gamble with the money." I can't help smiling. "She wanted to try counting cards."

"She's a card shark?"

I snort. "Not at all. She's just good with numbers."

Dad shakes his head. "Any casino would have made her in a heartbeat."

"Yeah, I told her."

"Sweet of her to want to try, though. That's a sweet girl right there."

"That's Savvy. She's the sweetest girl in the world."

"I'd like to meet her. Why don't we do a double date in LA?"

"I don't know, Dad. Savvy and I might wind up saying our goodbyes here in Vegas."

Dad looks surprised. "But you just said she's the sweetest girl in the world."

"It's complicated."

"Is she married or something?"

"No. It's just bad timing."

Dad rolls his eyes. "Look, son, I know you're young and on the prowl, and girls can't get enough of you. It was the same for me at twenty-four. But you can't play the field forever. If you find yourself a really sweet girl like Savvy, then grab her because you never know—"

"I'm not playing the field, Dad. I'm not on the prowl. You always think that about me, and I keep telling you I'm not like that. That's *you*, not me. *You* can't keep your dick in your pants. I manage it just fine. It's just complicated with Savvy, okay? Let's just leave it at that."

"What the fuck is so complicated? I saw your face when you were talking about her. Now stop over-thinking things and get out of your own way. You always think and think, Aidy. To a fault. It's not good for the brain to think so much. Follow your goddamned gut on occasion, Aidy. For the love of fuck."

"I met Savvy two days ago, Dad. My gut is hardly trustworthy on the topic."

"So what if you met her two days ago? You know what you *feel*."

"But what I'm feeling can't be real. I can't make any promises to a girl I met two days ago. Not this fast."

Dad narrows his eyes. "Who said anything about promises?"

"Savvy's not the kind of girl to string along."

"Ah, I get it. So you're just gonna push this girl away like you push everyone else away, huh? You're gonna be the lone wolf, yet again."

"I don't push everyone away. I just don't like letting people get too close. It's easier that way on everyone, in case things don't work out." I rake my hand through my hair. "She's squeaky clean, Dad. She went to Stanford. Obviously, she doesn't need a guy like me in her life."

Dad squints at me for a long moment. He takes a bite of his food. Chews it slowly. "Okay. I get it. And I agree. Fuck Savvy. She's sweet but she doesn't need a loser like you in her life."

I take a bite of my food. "I didn't say I'm a *loser*," I mumble. "I just said she's too good for me."

"Got it." He takes a big bite of his toast. "Hey, you know what you should do?" He motions to Savvy's white SUV out the window in the parking lot. "You should hawk Savvy's car and take the money to that museum and beg them to let you buy back your guitar. I know a guy who fences cars without the pink slip. A nice SUV like hers, you could probably get enough money to convince them to—"

"I'm not gonna sell Savvy's car out from under her," I snap. But then I look around and lower my voice. "What the hell kind of asshole do you think I am? I just finished telling you Savvy rolled the dice that saved your life. And then she let me borrow her fucking car to come buy your freedom. You think I'd let her save your life and help me like that and then turn around and fuck her over?"

Dad shrugs. "Hey, you just met her two days ago. You said so yourself. She can't possibly mean more to you than Betty. So why not sell her car and head straight to the museum? It's worth a try."

"You just finished telling me you and Bethany got struck by lightning the first time you met."

"We did."

"So you get to find the perfect girl and have some kind of white picket fence with her while I find the perfect girl and treat her like shit?"

"What do my feelings for Bethany have to do with your feelings for Savvy? You didn't feel a lightning bolt with her, did you? She's just a sweet girl you met in a bar. She could leave you next week, for all you know, just like everyone else has always left you at one point or another. So why would you want to risk getting left by someone you care about, *again*, when you could head to that museum and try to buy back a guitar you *know* will always treat you right?"

I lean back in my chair, realization dawning on me. "Holy shit. You're doing that thing you do, aren't you?"

Dad smiles wickedly.

I shake my head, but I can't help returning his smile.

"Did it help you figure things out?" Dad asks.

I grab my coffee mug. "Fuck you. And yes."

Dad laughs. "You're welcome." He brings his mug to

his lips to cover his cocky smile. "Now finish your breakfast, dumbshit. You're gonna need to fuel up so you can show Savvy an extra good time this afternoon."

I take a huge bite of my eggs. "You're good."

"I am. Especially when it comes to you." He winks. "I can read you like a book, son."

I feel electrified. *Free.* Thanks to Dad's manipulations, I suddenly know what to do about the Regina-Betty-Savvy situation—because I know exactly what I want. "I would have figured my shit out without you playing armchair psychologist," I say. "Don't give yourself too much credit, old man."

Dad shrugs like he doesn't believe a word of it, his eyes twinkling.

"So tell me more about Bethany," I say, bringing my coffee mug to my lips. "She's got a jewelry business?"

"Yeah. You should see the stuff she makes. It's beautiful. She designs everything, all by herself, and then she solders it together. She's a true artist."

"Is jewelry her day job?"

"Not yet, but that's the dream. She's a cocktail waitress at the Golden Nugget for now, just because she's got her son to support, but—"

"*She's got a son?*"

A huge smile spreads across Dad's face. "Austin. He's four. Cutest little bugger you ever saw. Smart as a whip, too. He's exactly how I'd imagine you must have been at the same age."

"Damn. She's moving fast with you, considering she's got a kid in tow."

"It's love, Aidy. Pure and simple. I told her I'm gonna do

whatever I have to do to take care of her and Austin 'til the end of time, and I'm gonna keep that promise, no matter what. For starters, I'm gonna be director of sales for her jewelry business and make big things happen for her."

"What do you know about jewelry?"

"Nothing. But I know I can sell ice to an Eskimo."

"True."

"Watch me. I'm gonna get Bethany's stuff into those fancy boutiques on Rodeo Drive or those hipster shops on Melrose. Hell, maybe I'll even get her stuff onto QVC. And if not, if the jewelry biz doesn't work out, then, okay, I'll figure something else out. A buddy of mine said he'd hire me as a bartender. I could do that. As long as I'm with Bethany and Austin, I'll be okay."

"Who are you?"

Dad chuckles. "I've already wasted enough time in my life. If this brush with death taught me anything, it's to seize the day."

My heart squeezes at the earnest look on my father's face. "I'm really happy for you, Dad."

"I'm really happy for me, too." He glances out the window of the diner toward the parking lot, and his face lights up. "Speak of the angel. Bethany's here. And it looks like she brought Austin, too."

I follow Dad's gaze just in time to see a blue sedan pulling into a parking spot.

"Come on, Aidy," Dad says. He rises from his chair, a smile on his face. "Come outside and meet my new family."

I glance at the clock and my stomach clenches. "I'll be

right there. Just need to make a quick phone call first."

CHAPTER TWENTY

AIDEN

Friday, 11:06 a.m.

After parking Savvy's car, I make my way on foot toward an area that seems like the heart of UNLV's campus. But, of course, it's just a guess, since I've never been to UNLV, let alone any college campus. I wander aimlessly through swarms of students for a few minutes and finally slip inside a building marked as Administration. Seems like a good place to start. Ten minutes and heaps of Southern charm later, I'm quietly sliding into a chair in the back row of a classroom, watching the professor write a string of numbers and symbols onto a white board underneath the phrase "Central Limit Theorem." The professor's back is turned as he writes, but even without seeing his face, I know I'm in the right place. The dude's got Savvy's exact hair. Plus, something in the way he moves reminds me of Savvy, too. *Bingo.*

Finally, the guy turns around to address the class, and my heart stops. Yup. That's most definitely Savvy's father. Professor Raymond Valentine. The man who shattered my little chicken girl's heart.

"So what do you think?" Savvy's father asks the class.

"Which version is superior? The Lyapunov version or the Lindeberg one?"

A student in the front row says something I can't understand—something about the "sum of lots of little random pieces behaving like the standard 'bell-shaped curve.'" And then a second student pipes in by saying, "But the Lindeberg condition can't be replaced by a still weaker one because Feller proved that it's not only a *sufficient* condition for the conclusion of the theorem to hold but also a *necessary* condition."

What the hell? That flew so far above my head, it might as well have been hooked to a jet engine.

"Excellent," Savvy's father says. He makes an adjustment to the string of notations on the whiteboard, and everyone in the class reacts like he just started throwing out free bags of weed. And it suddenly occurs to me Savvy must be more than just book smart. She must be a literal genius if even half this shit makes sense to her.

Fifteen minutes later, Savvy's father wraps up class, and all around me, students begin packing up their backpacks. I watch and wait as Savvy's father gathers his stuff and finally walks up the aisle toward me, heading toward the exit to my left.

"Hi, Professor Valentine," I say as he approaches. I move into the aisle in front of him to stop his progress. "Could I talk to you for a minute?"

"You'll have to come to office hours later this afternoon," he says. "I've got a department meeting."

"It's about Savvy."

Boom. I've got his full attention. "Savvy sent you?"

"No. She doesn't know I'm here."

"Is she okay? Is something wrong?"

"Savvy's fine. Physically, anyway. Can we go somewhere to talk privately?"

Savvy's father looks distressed. "Follow me."

I follow him to a small office on the second floor of the building and take the seat he offers me. I say, "I came because I've been spending a lot of time with your daughter lately, and I know for a fact she really misses you."

"Savvy told you that?"

"Not with words. But she wears the ring you gave her for her sixteenth birthday. That little ruby heart? She said it's her most-prized possession."

Anguish grips the man's face. "Savvy told me never to contact her again. She said if she wants to see me, she knows where to find me. I've respected her wishes because I've already hurt her enough. But I think about her every day." He pulls a set of keys out of his pocket to reveal a smiling photo of Savvy on his key ring. "I look at this every single day. All I want to do is pick up the phone to call her, but she was very clear with me she wanted me to leave her alone."

I roll my eyes. "Savvy didn't tell you to leave her alone because she actually *wanted* you to leave her alone. At least, not *forever*. Yeah, she might have wanted some space in the beginning. But what she really wanted—or, at least, what she clearly wants now—is for you to try to win her over. She wants to know she's got the kind of father who loves her so much, he'd slay any dragon to win her back."

Savvy's father presses his lips together. He hangs his

head. "I never meant to hurt Savvy. If I could rewind time and do things differently, I would." He lifts his head and looks at me with pained, glistening eyes. "I know I must seem like a monster to you, based on what Savvy told you. But please believe me; the situation with Savvy's mother wasn't nearly as black and white as it seemed to Savvy. Savvy doesn't know this, of course, but her mother and I hadn't been intimate in years when I met Susannah, and we'd both agreed to—"

"Stop," I say, putting my hand up. "Please. I don't have a lot of time. I came here for one reason only: to tell you Savvy is in town until Sunday morning for her high school reunion."

Emotion washes over his face.

"She's here, man," I say. "It's time to pull your head out of your ass and contact her. She's got a daddy-sized hole in her heart. It's a hole only you can fill, unfortunately. Only you."

"You think she'll agree to see me?"

"No. I don't, actually. Which is why you're going to show up unannounced. I think it's fifty-fifty she'll slam the door in your face, to be honest, but you owe it to her to try. Even if she slams the door in your face, then at least she'll know you cared enough to try. Fight for her, man. That's all she wants. She wants to feel *wanted*. She wants to feel loved."

"I *do* love Savvy. With all my heart. How could I not? To know Savvy is to love her." He half-smiles. "But you obviously already know that. You wouldn't be here if you didn't already know that."

I feel my face flush crimson. "Yeah, she's the best."

"I just hope she can find it in her heart to forgive me. I didn't mean to fall in love with Susannah. I wanted to be in love with Savvy's mother, Greta. But I wasn't. Greta got pregnant with Savvy when we were very young and—"

"Like I said, it's none of my business. Believe me, I'm not in any position to judge you or anyone else, Professor. I just came to tell you Savvy is staying at the Bellagio."

"What room number?"

"Twenty-one forty-seven. If she's in the room tonight at seven, could you come then?"

"I'll be there. Seven sharp."

"Good." I get up and head toward the door. "See you then."

"Hey," he says behind me, stopping my movement. "You never told me your name."

"Aiden."

"Thank you, Aiden. Savvy is lucky to have a boyfriend who loves her as much as you so obviously do."

My cheeks flushing, I nod. "See you tonight." With that, I swing open the door and march down the hallway.

CHAPTER TWENTY-ONE

SAVANNAH

Friday, 12:07 p.m.

As I pace back and forth in my hotel room, my hair wet from my shower, I glance at the clock on the nightstand for the fourteenth time in seven minutes. Well, there's no denying it now. Aiden isn't coming back. He most definitely reported for duty with the birthday girl. So much for my brilliant plan of insisting he take my car this morning. Was he so mortified at the thought of telling me about his decision that he decided to drop off my keys at the front desk downstairs? Will a hotel staffer come knocking at my door any minute, my keys in hand?

I glance at the clock again, despite not wanting to do it, and my heart pangs sharply. *12:08*. Should I call him? Aiden and I never exchanged cell numbers. We've been attached at the hip since the moment we laid eyes on each other, so why would we think to swap numbers? But there was a phone number associated with his name when I ran that background check on him. Should I use it? What would I even say to him if I called, besides, *Hey, Aiden, where's my freaking car?* I suppose I could tell him that, ten minutes after he left this morning, I had an epiphany that rocked my world—an idea about how to get his guitar back. But if I revealed that to him, wouldn't that come off like nothing but a pathetic ploy to buy his affection?

I rub my forehead, still pacing around my room. No, I can't call him. If he didn't come back to me on his own, I don't want him. If he didn't come back, it's because he's decided he values his guitar more than he values pursuing a potential relationship with me. And I can't blame him, really. We barely know each other, after all. This intense connection we're having can't possibly be real, can it? Plus, if I were to call him and tell him my idea, and he were to come back to me *solely* because I've possibly figured out a way to get his guitar back, then how would that make me feel? Like shit, that's how. No, thanks.

I glance at the clock again. *12:12.*

And it's not like I can *guarantee* my big idea will work. I need time to figure out a whole bunch of stuff before I'll know for sure. Am I willing to call Aiden now and beg him to leave a sure thing—the birthday girl—and then find out tomorrow my big idea went bust?

Plus, I'm not sure if I'm willing to pursue my idea for Aiden, anyway—not if he's not certain about his feelings for me. My idea is *illegal*, after all. Am I willing to go out on a limb for a guy who doesn't want me for me? No, I'm not. I mean, yeah, I know Aiden *wants* me. A guy can't fake the kind of passion Aiden has shown me. But if he's not coming back, then he clearly doesn't want me more than he wants that guitar. And I'm not going to subject myself to potential legal exposure, no matter how small, for a guy who doesn't want me as desperately and passionately as I want him.

12:16.

Okay, now I'm really wondering where the hell he is. He's got my car, after all. Oh, shit. Did Aiden steal my freaking car? I clutch my chest at the thought. Is he halfway to LA right now in my car, laughing about how stupid I was to hand him my keys? I gasp. Is Aiden going to *sell* my car in LA and use the money to buy back his guitar? My heart lurches. He wouldn't do that, would he? *Oh, Savvy. Stupid, stupid Savvy.*

I open my laptop and run a search and easily discover my SUV is worth about twenty-seven-thousand bucks on the used market. *Holy shit.* Was Aiden playing me all along? Was he brazenly charming my stupid, gullible ass this whole time with the goal of getting me to hand over my keys? No, no, no. I simply won't believe it. If Aiden wanted to steal my car, he could have done it twenty times before this morning. Plus, come on. There's no way Aiden was faking his chemistry with me just to steal my car. I have to believe he's made arrangements to get my car keys back to me. Unless...

I gasp. Is Aiden hurt? Did the bad guys at the motel beat him...or *worse*? Panic floods me. *Aiden.* Okay, that's it. I'm calling him.

My hands shaking, I grab my laptop, navigate into Aiden's background check report, and call the phone number listed at the top. Immediately, an automated outgoing message begins—a computerized voice that tells me the number I've reached and then instructs me to leave a message at the beep.

I grip the phone with white knuckles and, at the sound of the beep, ramble the following pathetic message: "Hi. This message is for Aiden MacAllister. I don't know if this is the right number for him. This is Savvy. Aiden, please, if you get this, call me. I'm worried something happened to you. I'm worried you're hurt. Please call or text to let me know you're okay. And, by the way, if you *are* okay, then, hey, motherfucker! Where's my car?" My tone is playful, but saying the words out loud brings tears to my eyes. I whisper, "Aiden, did you steal my car? Did you report for duty with Regina? Are you dead?" I blink and tears squirt down my cheeks. "If you went to the birthday girl's room at noon," I say, my stomach churning. "If I'm truly never going to see you again, Aiden, then, please..." I take a deep breath. "Just know that...." I swallow hard again. "The past forty-eight hours have been the best of my life." I press my lips together, trying not to lose it. "If you're not coming back, then leave my car keys at the front desk, okay? Because I'd like to head back to LA today, as soon as possible. But, either way, even if you're stealing my car right now and laughing your ass off at what an idiot I am, then at least text me to tell me you're alive so I won't worry about you. I'd rather be angry at you than worry you're lying dead in a ditch." I take a deep breath, fighting not to break down into pitiful sobs. "Goodbye, Aiden. I hope you're okay." I disconnect the call and lower my head...and break down into racking, pitiful sobs...just as my phone pings with an incoming text.

CHAPTER TWENTY-TWO

SAVANNAH

My heart leaping, I check the screen on my phone, irrationally thinking the incoming text is somehow from Aiden, even though I know he doesn't have my phone number. But, nope. It's a text from Kyle.

Bad news, Savage. I'm not gonna make it to LV. ☹ Just found out I have to babysit a band in NYC on Sat. night. The drummer and lead singer want to kill each other, and that's not a figure of speech, so my boss asked me to hang with them backstage to make sure nobody pulls a knife. Consolation prize? I'll for sure be in LA next month and I PROMISE to see you then. Be sure to tell Mason C to fuck off for me at the reunion. I'm sorry I won't be there to do it myself. Forgive me! I love youuuu! XOXOXO

My chest still heaving with sobs after my voicemail to Aiden, I tap out a reply to Kyle.

All is forgiven, my darling dearest.

Duty calls. But I won't be telling Mason
C to fuck off because I'm not going to the
reunion. Heading back to LA today. My
give-a-shitter done broke. Can't wait to
see you next month. Love you, tooooo.
XOXO

I press send, drop my phone onto the mattress next to me, and hang my head. And when my gaze lands on my hands in my lap and onto my ruby ring, despair gives way to a torrent of rage and hurt and rejection. I leap off the bed, yank the cursed ring off my finger, and hurl it across the room with a loud howl. *Goddamnit!* I'm done getting my heart trampled!

I crumple onto the edge of the bed and cover my face with my hands. Why, oh why, did I let myself get so attached to Aiden? He flat-out told me he'd tell me goodbye. He was clear he'd do *anything* he had to do when he got to Vegas. So why did I think, even for a second, Aiden would forego a *sure-fire* way to get his guitar back in order to pursue the *possibility* that our connection *might* turn out to be the real deal?

I lift my head, my eyes wide with an epiphany. Aiden didn't come back to me because he doesn't believe we'd work out in the end...*because he thinks I'm too good for him.* So why should he lose his beloved guitar for a girl he's sure he won't wind up with? It makes perfect sense. Which means I shouldn't take any of this personally. He's just not equipped to believe in fairytales.

All of a sudden, I want nothing more than to help Aiden get his fairytale, even if I won't be there to witness it. Assuming he's not lying in a ditch right now, that is. *Gah.* No, I can't think that way. I have to believe he's alive and well and simply decided to go to Regina's room because he couldn't allow himself to believe in miracles.

Well, guess what? I don't need Aiden to believe in *us*, for me to believe in *him*.

I grab my laptop, navigate to YouTube, copy the links to my three favorite Aiden Jameson videos, and paste them into a text message to Kyle.

> *Heyyyy! Forgot to tell you: I met an amazing musician the other day, right after my hike. Check out the links for Aiden Jameson. He's the grandson of Mac MacAllister, a legendary session musician from Nashville. Super talented and VERY easy on the eyes. He plays guitar and piano and sings and writes songs. Swoon! He does session work in LA, so keep him in mind if you hear of an opportunity. Pleeeeease take a look at these links! You'll be glad you did!*
> *XOXOXO*

I press send on my text, toss my phone onto the bed, and stare at the wall for a long moment, my heart aching. But when I happen to glance at the clock again—and realize it's now absolutely, positively, irrefutably one thousand percent certain I'll never see Aiden again as long as I live, I put my hands over my face and let loose with a sob from the depths of my soul... just as the door to the room swings open, and Aiden bursts into the room.

CHAPTER TWENTY-THREE

AIDEN

The instant I see Savvy crying on the bed, I know she didn't get the voicemail I left for her on the room phone—and a quick glance at the desk confirms as much: the little red light on the phone is blinking.

"Savvy," I say, barreling to her and taking her into my arms. "*Baby.*"

She throws her arms around me and crumples against my chest and wails.

"It's okay, chicken girl," I whisper, holding her to me and stroking her hair. Oh, God, the sound of her crying is breaking my heart. "Sh, baby. I'm here."

"I thought I'd never see you again," she says between sobs. "I thought you were hurt. Or dead. Or that you went to that woman's hotel room to—"

"No, baby, no. I couldn't go through with it. Of course, not. Not *now.*" I kiss her hair. Her temple. Pull back and kiss her salty cheeks. "I left you a message on the room phone. I didn't want you to worry."

Savvy looks at the phone on the desk and sees the flashing red light. "I...I must have been in the shower when you called."

"And you didn't notice the red light when you got out?"

"It's been flashing since we got to the room. I figured it was an automated welcome message." She wipes her eyes. "I left you a message, too. At least, I think I did."

"Oh, I've had my phone off." I pull out my phone.

"Just delete it," she says quickly.

"What'd you—"

"Nothing. I just babbled pathetically. Please delete it, okay? I was worried you were hurt. I wasn't thinking clearly."

I'm curious what she said in her message, but she looks so damned anxious, I quickly delete the message.

She sighs with relief. "Thank you. What did you say in your message to me?"

I motion to the phone on the desk. "You can listen to it, if you want."

Savvy moves to the desk and puts the phone on speaker mode. She logs into the voicemail system and presses a button and a canned female voice blares on the line. "Welcome to the Bellagio! We hope you enjoy your stay at—" She presses a button and, after a brief pause, my voice comes on and says, "Hey, Savvy, it's me."

My skin pricks to hear the obvious emotion straining my tone.

My voicemail message continues. "We never exchanged phone numbers, so I'm calling here. I just wanted to let you know the meet-up with my father went perfectly. I'll tell you about it in person. I'm on my way to run an errand and didn't want you to worry if it runs long or if traffic back to the Strip is horrible. I texted the birthday girl and told her the job is off.

Actually, I told her to go fuck herself. I'll probably be back at the room around noon or so, but if not, don't go anywhere, okay?" I pause on the line. "Savvy, I want to see where this thing between us might lead in the real world. And in the meantime, if you're still looking for a date for your reunion, then I volunteer as tribute." I chuckle softly on the line. "I'll see you soon, sweetheart. I can't wait to kiss you and hold you in my arms and say all this stuff to you in person. So stay put in the room, okay? And don't worry about me. I'm fine and coming back to the room as soon as I can get there. Bye."

The line goes dead.

Savvy looks at me, her eyes wide and lips parted. "Well, shit," she says. "That would have been an awfully nice message to get."

CHAPTER TWENTY-FOUR

AIDEN

My euphoric kiss with Savvy quickly becomes one of deep passion. Desperation. *Urgency.* In a frenzy of heat and want and *need*, we disrobe and begin mauling each other. I lay her naked body down on the bed and reach between her legs—and moan when I discover how wet and swollen she is for me. My heart racing and my dick throbbing, I begin massaging Savvy's hard tip as I continue kissing her. And within minutes, I'm rewarded with the sensation of her muscles rippling against my hand. Oh, God, I want to burrow inside this woman. But I resist. Because, in this moment, even more than I crave my own pleasure, I crave Savvy's.

I shift my fingers and begin stroking her G-spot with firm, confident strokes—and it's instantly clear my touch is sending her straight to heaven.

"Aiden," Savvy growls, riding my hand. Her eyelids are half-mast. Her cheeks are in full bloom. She looks absolutely drugged with arousal. *And I love it.*

How did I waffle even for a moment about my decision? Because now that I'm here with this girl, my heart leaping and soaring at her every moan and whimper, it's clear to me there was never an actual choice to be made. This woman owns me. I don't know how. Or where we go from here. Or if we'll even have any kind of actual future, given how different we are, but in this moment, the only thing my heart is telling me is I belong here with her.

"Aiden," Savvy says again. But that's all she's going to say, apparently. She's a woman on the edge of rapture. Quickly, I grab my phone next to me on the mattress and record her face. Her eyes rolling back into her head. The way her eyebrows knit together like she's in pain.

"Come for me, baby," I coo. "I'm recording."

A hard suck on her nipple and a couple more swipes of her G-spot, and Savvy inhales sharply, throws her head back, and comes against my hand.

When she's done, I prop my phone against a pillow, still recording, and crawl greedily on top of her, pull her hands over her head, weave my fingers in hers, and burrow inside her, all the fucking way to my balls, and fuck her hard with everything I've got.

"Yes," Savvy purrs underneath me as I fuck her. She wraps her thighs around me, and we both growl and groan with pleasure at the sensation of our bodies igniting.

"You've ruined me," I grit out.

"I don't want anyone else," she whispers.

A tidal wave of pleasure rises sharply inside me, threatening to crash down, but I don't want to let go yet. I want this electricity I'm feeling in this moment to last forever.

"Get on top," I growl. "I want to watch you."

We maneuver until she's riding me, licking her lips,

touching her breasts. I grab the phone and record her breasts softly bouncing as she fucks me, the curve of her hips, the fall of her dark hair around her milky shoulders. When she throws her head back, gracing me with a view of her long neck and erect nipples, I jolt and buck underneath her, on the verge of total ecstasy.

"You're gorgeous," I say, still pointing the camera at her. "Look straight into the camera for me."

She follows my command. She looks straight at the camera, grabs my free hand, slides my index finger into her mouth, and begins sucking and licking it.

"Oh, fuck, that's hot," I say. I throw the phone down, sit up, and cradle her in my arms, holding on to her for dear life as she fucks me hard and fast. Finally, she throws her head back, juts her hard nipples toward me, digs her nails into my shoulders, and comes like a freight train—so hard, I feel wetness trickling down my balls. With a loud roar, I release, gripping her back hard as waves of pleasure rack through me.

When I'm able to breathe again, I grab Savvy's face and kiss her passionately, my heart racing and my soul flying. Finally, we pull away from devouring each other and flop onto the bed, our chests heaving and our bodies sweaty. We rearrange ourselves until we're lying entangled on the bed, caressing and stroking each other. And we talk. I tell her the harrowing story of what happened in the motel room when I paid for my father's freedom. I tell her about my father's plan to live in LA with his new girlfriend and her son. And I tell her how ecstatic I am to be here with her right now.

"What did Regina say when you told her to go fuck

herself?" Savvy asks.

"I didn't give her the chance to reply. I sent her a text and blocked her number."

Savvy giggles with glee and snuggles into my chest. "Oh, Aiden. I'm so glad you came back to me. So, so glad."

"Me, too, baby. Me, too."

"What finally made you decide to come back?"

I stroke Savvy's hair, considering my words. On the one hand, I don't want to over-promise. No matter what I'm currently feeling—or think I'm currently feeling—I can't let myself forget I've known this girl for two measly days. On the other hand, though, I want her to understand I'm feeling something incredible with her. Something I've never felt before. "I just imagined myself playing Betty. I thought about how I'd feel playing her, knowing I'd sacrificed my integrity to get her back. Knowing I'd given up any shot I might have had with you." I run my fingertips down Savvy's naked back, and I take a deep breath. "And I realized the price was just too high to get Betty back."

Savvy lifts her head. Her eyes are sparkling. She smiles broadly.

"I can't make you any promises," I say softly, still stroking her back. "I have no idea what's going to happen with us when we get back to LA—if these feelings will survive in real life. But I know I've never felt this way before with anyone else. Not even close. And I know I want to be worthy of the way you always look at me."

"I've never felt this way, either. I didn't even *know* I could feel this way." She kisses me gently, and when she pulls back, she's beaming with joy. "Aiden, there's something I've been dying to tell you since you walked through the door. I think I've figured out a way to get Betty back!"

CHAPTER TWENTY-FIVE

AIDEN

Friday, 1:44 p.m.

"My boss told me I was one of four people being considered for promotion to team manager," Savvy explains. "And, man, I wanted that promotion."

We're lying side-by-side on the bed, fully dressed. Savvy's got her laptop on her belly. As she speaks, she's navigating into something on her computer—a memo she says will help explain this "big idea" of hers for getting Betty back.

"So I got ambitious," Savvy continues. "On my own time, I started secretly auditing the production control systems of the company's biggest corporate clients. I was looking for vulnerabilities—you know, ways they could get hacked—and as I did my research, I wrote up a detailed memo about my findings. I was planning to turn in the memo at the end of the month and impress the hell out of the decision-makers regarding the promotion." She makes a snarky face. "But then I got shitcanned before I'd had the chance to say a word about it to anyone." She motions to her computer and flashes a devious smile. "Which means nobody, other than you and me, knows this memo—this *blueprint*—exists."

I glance at her screen, but I can't make heads or tails of it. "I don't understand. How is it a blueprint? For what? Some kind of hacking? Your plan is for us to hack something?"

"Correct. Well, my plan begins with a hack and ends with a sort of a heist."

"A *heist*?" I rub my forehead. "Savvy, no. I can't let you—"

"Aiden. Please. Just listen. My idea is almost foolproof. Let me explain it."

"Start at the beginning."

She looks giddy. "The corporations I audited were in a variety of industries: banks, big-box retailers, national restaurant chains...and *casinos*. Almost fifty casinos, actually. Fifteen of them right here on the Strip. Including the casino at this hotel." She motions to her laptop. "This memo details how hackers might penetrate the backbones of all the companies I audited, including the casinos. Which means, if put into the wrong hands, the memo would become somewhat of an instruction manual. A step-by-step guide to infiltrating those corporations' systems."

"For what purpose?"

"Patience, Grasshopper. I'm getting there. When I got my big epiphany after you left this morning, I poked around to see if anyone has, by chance, plugged up the holes I found in my audit. And they haven't. Not a single vulnerability I found has been discovered or addressed by anyone. Which means I've still got detailed step-by-step instructions on how to access those fifteen casinos on the Strip. Specifically, I found a vulnerability in the backchannel that the gaming regulatory commission uses to monitor all of the Nevada casinos. A way into all of them, pretty much all at once, sidestepping all of their firewalls." She pats her computer. "And it's all right here."

My heart is beating like a steel drum. "But how will accessing the systems of fifteen casinos lead to us pocketing twenty-five grand? Are you planning to steal credit card numbers from their databases? Transfer money out of the casinos' bank accounts? Because there's no way in hell I'm going to let you do anything that's—"

"No, no. It's nothing pedantic like outright thievery. Nothing so *obvious*." She rolls her eyes. "We're not going to directly *steal* the money. That would be too risky. Not to mention immoral." She grins. "We're going to hack into their systems, get particular information we need, and then use that information to gamble and *win* the money, fair and square." She snickers. "Except it won't be fair and square, of course, because we'll have rigged the game in our favor. But that's a minor immorality I can live with."

Goose bumps erupt on my arms. *Holy shit.* "Which game?"

Savvy pauses for effect, excitement overtaking her pretty features. "*Slots.*"

I can't help feeling deflated. I don't know which game I thought she was going to say, but it certainly wasn't slots. "We're going to try to win twenty-five grand playing *slots*?"

Savvy nods. "We sure are. When I poke around the casinos' systems, I can get the complete payout histories of every single slot machine on the casinos' floors. And from that data, I can surmise which machines have paid out recently and which haven't. And from *that* data, I'm pretty sure I'll be able to extrapolate payout patterns and determine, with statistical certainty, which machines are 'hot.'"

My shoulders sag. *Shit*. For a second there, I let myself get excited. "Sweetheart, I know you're trying to help me," I say. "And I really appreciate that. But this all sounds incredibly far-fetched. Or as Gramps used to say 'like a bunch of hooey.'"

"It's not 'hooey.' It's simple math. I admit I don't have the capability to predict payouts yet, but I believe, if I create the right algorithm to analyze the information, I'll be able to do it the vast majority of the time. Now, admittedly, the plan isn't foolproof. The algorithm will be based on statistical probabilities, so there will be anomalies, etcetera. And I also admit there are some practical considerations that might throw a monkey wrench in the works, or at least lower our odds. I'll be creating an algorithm that will make predictions—but, yes, there will be a margin of error. But, regardless of all that, over the course of, say, a hundred machines, it's my belief the chances are well over eighty percent we'll be able to win twenty-five grand. I just need some time to gather data and create the algorithm and off we go."

"What are the practical considerations? You said there are practical considerations that might throw a monkey wrench in the works?"

"I see a couple things. First off, single payouts of twelve hundred bucks or more have to be reported for taxes. We'd have to fill out tax forms with the casino, including showing identification, to get our winnings." She makes a sour face. "That's a firm no, obviously. Which means we can't win more than eleven-hundred-ninety-nine bucks on any given machine."

"Would it be possible to cap winnings like that? It seems hard enough to predict a winning machine in the first place."

"Honestly, making sure we stay under the reporting threshold on every win is going to be the hardest part of this whole idea. I mean, obviously, keeping our winnings below a desired amount would be a simple function of the amount we bet. You can only win so much on a twenty-dollar bet versus a hundred-dollar bet, for instance. But how do we keep things under twelve hundred while still ensuring we win enough each bet to make it worth our while? We don't want to waste the golden opportunity of a hot machine by winning a hundred bucks, you know? Getting to twenty-five grand would take way too long to make your deadline with the museum if we don't win around a grand each and every time. We'd want to stay under the radar but also get in and out as quickly as possible to lessen our risk of attracting attention."

I run my hand through my hair. "Frankly, this sounds like a tall order, baby. I'm sorry to be negative, but this sounds like a pipe dream."

"It's not. It's not going to be easy, but I can do it. It's nothing but a math and coding problem, Aiden. I've got this."

"A math and coding problem, sure, but you said *two* practical considerations. What's the second one?"

"I'm almost positive I'll be able to identify the hottest machines at any given time, but the landscape could change on a dime. What if I've zeroed in on a particular slot but some random person plays it and wins before we get there? Or what if someone is playing our machine when we get there? We can't very well ask someone to leave. We'd have to move to another machine. Which means I'd need to watch-dog the systems in real time to make sure we're not dealing with stale information from minute to minute."

I shake my head, overwhelmed. "This is too risky. There are too many moving parts."

"No, no. All of these variables are containable. I'm sure of it. I just need some time to work the problem. It's a puzzle, Aiden. And I love solving puzzles. It's what I *live* for."

"Okay, puzzle me this: assuming all of this is possible, just like you're saying, where would we get the seed money to get started? Your ring, I presume?"

"Correct. I can get at least two grand for it. And that's all we need to get started."

"Then my answer is a firm no. For all the reasons I said before, I won't let you hawk your ring for me."

"It's not up to you, Aiden. I'm going to do this whether you want me to or not. I'm going to create my algorithm and see if my idea works, simply because I won't be able to sleep at night if I don't at least try this idea. The only question is whether you're in or out. I hope you're in because things will go a whole lot faster if you're on the casino floors playing the slots, but, even if you're not in, I'm doing this."

"You're bluffing," I say. "And not very well, I might add."

"I'm not."

"You already told me you need to watch-dog the systems. You can't do that and play the slots at the same time. Which means you can't possibly do this alone. You need me to pull this off. Which means I *do* have a say. *And I say no.* I really appreciate you wanting to help me, but I won't let you sell that ring for a longshot like this."

"But I'm not going to *sell* it. I'm going to offer it to a pawn shop as collateral for a short-term loan. And when we've won enough money for me to buy it back, I'll waltz back into the pawn shop and buy it back."

"Best laid plans, baby," I say. I grab her hand, intending to make a point about her ring, and jolt when I discover she's not wearing it. "You already hawked it? *Savvy!*"

She looks down at her hand. "Oh. No. I hurled it across the room." She smiles sheepishly. "I had a bit of a meltdown when I thought you weren't coming back."

"Aw, chicken girl." I touch her cheek. "I'm so sorry you thought that."

"It's all right. When you walked through the door, the jolt of pure joy I felt more than made up for the pain." She beams a wide smile at me. "I threw it that way. Will you help me find it?"

We both begin searching the floor for the ring.

"I just thought of another practical consideration," I say, my eyes scanning the carpet for that little ruby heart. "Even if your algorithm works, how can we be sure we won't run out of our seed money before we've hit pay dirt on our first slot? We could play every dollar of the ring money on a 'hot slot' without getting a hit, and the very next player on the machine could waltz up and hit a jackpot."

"True, but... Ah! Found it," she says. She straightens up, holding her ring, a huge smile on her face.

"Honey, seriously. Thank you for wanting to do this, but this whole plan has more holes in it than a sieve."

"I never said it was ironclad. I said from the start we'd be playing the statistical probabilities. The only difference is I'd make sure the statistical probabilities were heavily stacked in our favor. But what the hell, Aiden? It's worth a try, right? Our give-a-shitters done broke, baby. Let's give it a whirl."

I chew my cheek. Damn, I'm tempted. But I can't stand the thought of her losing that ring for me.

"Take a leap of faith with me, Aiden," she says. "All the raw data I need is just sitting there, waiting for me." She grabs my hand. "*Trust me.*"

"I do trust you. But you said yourself there are elements outside your control here. Plus, there are things you haven't considered."

"Like what?"

"Well, for one thing, there are video cameras everywhere. Floor supervisors. We're going to need to make sure we stay under the radar. That part isn't math or coding. That's just good-old-fashioned *grifting.* And that's not your strong suit, Savvy Who Isn't Savvy. No offense."

"None taken. But that's exactly why we're such a great team. I'm going to figure out how to beat the house from a mathematical perspective, and you're going to figure out how we'll get away with it."

My mind is racing. I must admit, I'm feeling a glimmer of hope this could work. "Okay. The most important thing here is we can't get greedy," I say. "In and out."

She nods.

"It helps that we're planning to keep our winnings at around a grand each time. That's not an amount that should attract any attention. But at that rate, winning thirty grand—twenty-five plus enough for you to buy back your ring—will take at least a couple days."

"More like three, would be my guess," she says. "Seeing as how we'll have to eat and sleep at some point."

"True." I bite my lip, thinking. "We definitely wouldn't want to stay at any one casino for too long. We'll need to rotate. Hit a jackpot at one casino, and move on to the next one."

"Okay," Savvy says. "But when you say 'we,' that's going to have to be you. Like I said, I'll need to stay online at all times to keep checking data in real time in the room. I'll watch the data and direct you to the next hot machine at whichever casino."

I sigh. "Three days is a really long time for one guy to be seen winning at slots again and again. Even if I'm rotating through different casinos on a loop, I'm a little nervous someone will make me."

Savvy twists her mouth, considering. "Yeah, good point. Especially when the guy hitting jackpot after jackpot has a face as memorable as yours. You're definitely not an average Joe, babe. I've noticed people stare at you wherever we go."

I roll my eyes. "They're staring at *you*."

She snorts.

"Look, I'd feel a whole lot better about this plan if we could switch off. If I could play the slots one day, and you could play them the next."

"It's not possible," Savvy says. "There's no way you could run command central. At any given time, the variables will change and different machines will go from 'hot' to 'dead' in the blink of an eye. My algorithms won't be user-friendly like an app on your iPhone."

I exhale with resignation.

"Don't worry, we'll figure this out," Savvy says. "The two of us combined make the world's most perfect brain, remember? A perfect team in a zombie apocalypse."

I rub my face with my hand. *Shit*. I want to believe this could work. But I'm nervous to get Savvy mixed up into something that could go south on her and literally ruin her entire life. "I'm nervous," I admit. "You're squeaky clean, baby. No matter what, I want to keep you that way."

"I'd cover my tracks. No one would ever know I was poking around inside these casinos' systems. I've got lots of tricks up my sleeve."

I don't reply, simply because I'm thinking too many competing thoughts.

"You don't buy the whole premise, do you?" Savvy says. "You don't think I can predict a hot machine, do you?"

"I'm sorry. I have faith in you. I do. But I don't see how that's possible. Aren't those machines designed to go off completely at random?"

"Yes, but randomness is a relative term. Take a coin toss, for example. It's totally random whether you'll get heads or tails on any given toss of a coin, right? You've got a fifty-fifty shot, and there's no way to predict with certainty what will happen. Plus, no matter the probabilities, it's possible that coin will come up heads ten straight times. But what if you flip that coin a hundred times? Even if your first ten tosses came up heads, that statistical aberration will likely have evened itself out over the course of a hundred flips. The more times you flip, the more likely it is you'll hit that fifty-fifty mark. And that's the kind of predictability we'll rely on here. The more machines we play, the more chance we'll have that everything will go according to plan. Our biggest risk is we hit an aberration on our very first machine and lose all our money, right off the bat. That's true. But I'm willing to take that risk."

I chew on the inside of my cheek. Everything she's saying is making sense to me, but I still can't wrap my head around her being able to predict when a slot machine will pay out...and then, on top of that, ensure that our winnings stay between a thousand and eleven hundred ninety-nine bucks each time.

Savvy lets out a long, deep sigh. "Okay, you obviously need a little convincing." She grabs her computer. Clacks on some keys. Furrows her brow. Clacks on a few more keys. And finally whispers, "*Perfect.*" She closes her computer, rises from the bed with her hand out, smiles, and says, "Come on, Aiden Who Isn't Easily Convinced. I'm going to show you proof of concept."

CHAPTER TWENTY-SIX

SAVANNAH

"That one on the end?" Aiden asks, pointing to a row of slot machines about twenty yards away from where we're standing in the noisy casino.

I look down at my phone, at the information I sent myself right before leaving our room. "No. The machine next to that one. The one that lady in purple is playing."

"How do you know she didn't already win on it while we were in the elevator coming down here?"

"I don't. I'd need to be sitting at my laptop, plugged into the Bellagio's system, to know for sure."

"Let's sit," Aiden says, motioning to two empty chairs in front of video poker consoles. "This could take a while."

We sit, our eyes trained like lasers on the woman in purple.

"You truly think that machine will go off any minute?" Aiden asks.

"I do, assuming it didn't go off in the few minutes it took us to get down here. If it's still hot, then, yes, I think it'll go off within the next twenty minutes or so, if I had to guess."

"What if we run into a situation like this when it counts— someone already sitting at our chosen machine?"

"Then we'll move onto another machine. There are hundreds of slots in every casino. If I get my algorithm right, then during any given hour, on a rotating basis, we'll have multiple machines to choose from. In fact, don't you think it would be good for other random people to win while we're winning, too? Won't that make us look less suspicious?"

"Yeah, but it will also prolong the con, which will prolong the risk we get noticed. Rule number one to a successful con? Get in and get out. The longer you're—"

Before Aiden can complete that sentence, the slot machine in front of the woman in purple lights up, and the woman throws up her hands. "I won!" she shrieks. "I won!"

Aiden looks at me, his mouth hanging open. "You're a genius."

I giggle with glee. "It's just math, like I said."

"Savvy, seriously, you're... Oh, my God. You're *literally* a genius, aren't you?"

I feel myself blushing. "Yes. But I'm nothing compared to my father. His IQ is ten points higher than mine."

Aiden shakes his head. "Savannah Valentine." He grabs my hand and lays a soft kiss on my knuckles. "You're beautiful, you know that?"

I can't stop smiling like a dope. "Thank you. So are you."

Aiden laughs. "Okay, my beautiful genius. You're going to get your brilliant mind up to our room and get crackin' on that algorithm. And while you're doing that, I'll hawk your ring and get you a turkey sandwich." He rubs his palms together and lets out a whoop of pure joy. "Let's get my beautiful guitar back, baby."

CHAPTER TWENTY-SEVEN

AIDEN

Friday, 6:52 p.m.

When I enter the room, I find Savvy sitting on the bed, staring intensely at her laptop, her brow furrowed.

"How's it going, Einstein?" I ask.

She looks up. "Good. I'm making excellent progress."

"You think you're pretty close?" I ask, crawling onto the bed next to her.

"I think so. There's just this one thing that's giving me fits. I need a little more time to noodle it, but I'm sure I can figure it out." She rubs her eyes. "Man, my eyes are crossing."

I move her computer off her lap and place it to the side. "You've been working nonstop for hours. Lie down and let me massage your shoulders."

"There's no time. If I'm going to lead command central while you hit the machines, it's going to take us three days to hit our target. That's cutting it awfully close for us to make it back to the museum in time on Monday."

"If time is getting short, we can fly back to LA and figure out how to get your car later. We'll figure it out, baby. Don't stress."

But she looks stressed. Highly stressed.

"Lie down, sweetheart," I say soothingly. "This isn't life or death. It's a guitar. Let me massage you and make it all better."

Sighing, she lies down on her side, and I begin massaging her stiff shoulders.

"Ah, that's nice. Thank you."

"The worst that can happen is Betty will live in a museum behind glass for the rest of her days, and the world will get to enjoy her. It won't be the end of the world."

"No, I'm getting that guitar back for you," she says firmly. "You said your grandfather's greatest wish was for you to play it for the rest of your life. He wouldn't have wanted Betty sitting untouched behind glass."

I sigh. Savvy is absolutely right. Gramps would have scoffed at the idea of Betty sitting behind glass like the crown jewels. He would have wanted her to *live*. To *sing*. But I've learned through a life filled with disappointments and losses never to hope for a miracle. Better to expect nothing and get pleasantly surprised if things work out...or to expect nothing at all and not feel too devastated when everything goes to shit.

"What were you doing all this time?" Savvy asks as I massage her.

"Killing time. After I hit the pawn shop and brought you your sandwich, I walked along the Strip for a while, just people watching and writing a song in my head. Oh, I bought a shirt. Then I found that catering manager and got into that storage room again. I worked out that song I'd been writing in my head for about three hours. And then I came back up here."

Savvy rearranges herself on the bed to face me. "I missed

you. Is that crazy? We've barely been apart since we met, and it felt weird being without you."

I grin. "I felt the same way."

We share a smile.

"So tell me about that thing that's been giving you fits," I say. "I won't be able to help you with it, of course. But maybe explaining it to me will somehow help you figure it out."

She twists her lips adorably, considering. "Well, the main thing I'm struggling with is—"

There's a knock at the door, and Savvy and I both look toward it.

"Who could that be?" she says.

I look at the clock on the nightstand. *7:00.* "Only one way to find out," I say, getting up from the bed.

"Wait," Savvy says sharply, halting my progress. She looks anxious. "What if it's Regina? What if she came here to offer you more money?" She puts her hand over her mouth. "Or what if it's one of the guys from the motel? What if someone followed you back here, and they're going to hurt you? Or kidnap me and demand ransom from you?"

Oh, my heart. I'll never forgive myself for dragging sweet little Savvy Valentine into this bullshit. "There's a peep hole," I say soothingly, walking toward the door. "I'll take a peek before I open the door, okay?"

"Be careful," she says, her voice tight.

I arrive at the door and peek through the hole to find Savvy's father on the other side of the door. "It's a middle-aged guy who looks strikingly like you."

"Huh?"

"Come see."

Savvy leaps off the bed and comes to the door. She peeks through the peep hole and gasps. *"It's my father!"* She clutches her chest. Her face flushes. "How the hell did he...?" She squints at me. "You invited him here?"

I nod. "I went to visit him this morning at UNLV after breakfast with my dad. That was my errand—the reason I was late coming back to the room."

Savvy wrings her hands. She looks like her brain is short circuiting.

Savvy's father knocks on the door again.

"Hang on, Professor!" I call through the door. I turn to Savvy. "Are you willing to see him?"

"I don't know."

"Sweetheart, you're still wearing the man's ring," I say. "Well, at least you were before I hawked it. That would suggest you should talk to him."

She looks down at her bare hand, and anxiety flickers across her face.

"If you don't like what he has to say, then tell him to leave. It's as simple as that."

She looks like her mind is going a mile a minute. But, finally, she nods...and I open the door.

CHAPTER TWENTY-EIGHT

A I D E N

Friday, 8:42 p.m.

I walk down the long hallway and arrive outside the door to our room. I don't know if Savvy and her dad are still in there. For all I know, Savvy's father left two minutes after I did. But I haven't heard from Savvy since I left hours ago, so I'm guessing she's still in there with her dad. I knock on the door. "Savvy?" I call out. "It's me."

"Come in," Savvy's voice says on the other side of the door.

I enter the room to find Savvy and her dad sitting at the small desk in the corner, huddled around her laptop. "Hey, you two."

Savvy looks up and smiles. "Hi," she says.

"How's it going?" I ask.

Father and daughter look at each other and grin shyly.

"Good," Savvy says. "We talked for a bit about everything. It was a productive conversation. A very good start." She looks reassuringly at her father before returning to me. "But then I told Dad I don't have time to deal with our relationship any more today because I'm working on an important and time-sensitive project."

"And I said, 'Well, if it's important to you, then it's important to me,'" Savvy's father chimes in to say.

"And that's when I realized Dad might be able to help me with the math for the algorithm! So I told him everything. I hope that's okay with you."

"That's fine."

She grins. "And guess what? My dad solved the problem that was giving me fits!" She squeals. "*The algorithm works!*"

"It wasn't a big deal," Savvy's father says. "I made the slightest adjustment to her calculations."

"An adjustment that made all the difference," Savvy says. She looks at me. "Thanks to my dad, we can now confidently predict which machines will pay *and* how much we'll need to bet to hit jackpots of between eight hundred to eleven hundred bucks."

"That's amazing," I say. My eyes drift to Savvy's hand... and I suddenly notice she's wearing her ruby ring again...even though I sold it to a pawn shop earlier today. "Your ring," I say.

Savvy smiles at her father. "Dad bought it back for me. He insisted. Actually, he tried to give me twenty-five grand, but I wouldn't take it. I hope you don't mind."

"I wouldn't have taken the money, either," I say. I look at Savvy's father. "Thank you for the offer, though."

"I'd do anything for Savvy," he says. "Which is why I'm going to play slots tonight along with you while Savvy stays up here in command central."

"Oh, wow. Thank you, but I can't drag you into this. You head up the math department at a major university."

"Savvy says the odds of us getting caught are slim. She's

going to cover her tracks brilliantly. Plus, if I help, I can increase productivity dramatically. We can divide and conquer and reach your goal in half the time—which means our exposure is cut down, too. Less time for one face to get caught winning over and over again. Less time out on the casino floor. It just makes sense for me to help."

I look at Savvy, not sure if I should accept this man's assistance or not.

"Aiden, Savvy explained how much you mean to her," Professor Valentine says. "And I've already seen for myself how much she means to you. If Savvy's going to do this—and she's made it clear to me she is, whether I like it or not—then I'd sleep better at night knowing I helped her get the job done twice as fast."

A tsunami of relief slams into me. I shouldn't let this guy help, but man, I can't resist. "Thank you so much, Professor. But here's a thought. If two guys playing slots will get us to our finish line twice as fast, why not add a third guy and get us there even faster? Three guys winning at fifteen casinos won't register as a blip on anybody's radar, right?"

"Your father?" Savvy asks.

"Yeah. He's not heading back to LA until Monday. And he's dying to pay me back somehow. He can be trusted."

Professor Valentine looks unsure, but Savvy's expression is one of pure elation.

"Fantastic," she says. "Call him."

"You're sure he can be trusted?" Professor Valentine says. And, suddenly, it's clear to me he knows everything about me and my father and our rap sheets.

I take a deep breath. "Please rest assured I'm a solid citizen these days, Professor," I say. "I haven't so much as jay-walked since I got out of prison. I helped my dad because he was gonna do it anyway, and I wanted to lower his risk of getting caught. I'm not a career criminal."

Professor Valentine smiles. "Savvy told me." He looks at his daughter. "And she also reminded me I'm in no position to judge anyone."

"I just want you to understand what we're doing here is a one-off," I say.

"Savvy told me that, too. And she also told me it was her idea, not yours."

"Well, yeah," I say. "I couldn't have come up with this idea if my life depended on it. I just want you to understand I've done bad things in my past, yes, but I'm not a bad person."

Savvy's father sighs. "Perhaps it's a self-serving philosophy, but I believe good people do bad things sometimes. And I also believe in forgiveness and second chances. If Savvy says you're worth taking this risk for, then I trust her. She's always been excellent at reading people."

Savvy and I both snort at the same time.

"Dad," Savvy says. "I'm *terrible* at reading people."

"No, you're not. You're wonderful at it."

Savvy giggles. "No. You're just horrifically bad at it."

I pull out my phone. "Is it okay for me to call my dad and tell him to come?"

"Call him," Savvy says.

"Cool. I'll tell him to pick up some burner phones on the way."

CHAPTER TWENTY-NINE

SAVANNAH

Saturday, 5:37 a.m.

Staring at my computer screen, I take a long gulp of coffee. I'm in the zone, baby. I put my cup down and clack on my keyboard for a moment—and, *voila*, the server terminal for Caesar's Palace opens before me like a beautiful, blooming rose. *Hello, gorgeous.*

A few more taps on my keyboard, and I've zeroed in on a hot machine for Aiden's dad, Nick, to play. Quickly, I create a diagram of the machine's precise location on the casino floor and text it to Aiden's father on his burner phone. But I've no sooner done that than I receive a text from Aiden on *his* burner phone telling me there's someone on the slot I directed him to at Mandalay Bay, and will I please send him an alternate assignment? Two seconds after that, I receive a text from my father saying his machine at Circus Circus is a dud, meaning it hasn't hit in the fifteen-minute window I've allotted for payouts before it's time to move on.

And so it goes. The same way things have gone all night long. Over and over again, I've tapped into the server of whichever casino for whichever guy, retrieved whatever required information, created a quick map of the machine's location, and sent the information off...only to get pulled in a completely different direction by someone else. It's been absolutely nonstop, all night long. Chaotic. Crazy-making. Thrilling. Exhausting. But, no doubt, productive. Because, hallelujah, the algorithm works. Is it perfect? No. There have been occasional duds, like what just happened with my father's machine. But that's not an aberration—that's something to be expected from a statistical standpoint. And there have been people sitting at our machines at times, too. But, again, we expected that. Indeed, I took squatters and duds into account when I calculated our odds of reaching twenty-five grand tonight at around seventy-two percent. "And, hey, if we don't reach our goal tonight, it's no biggie," I told everyone before they headed off to fight the good fight. "Aiden and I will simply pull a second shift as a duo tomorrow night and cross the finish line then."

As crazy as it sounds, I don't know how much we've won so far tonight. Up here in command central, there's about a thirty-second delay before I can see that a certain machine in the casino has hit, but even then, I can't see the *amount* paid out for another hour or so, depending on the reporting protocol of the particular server. And so, given how busy I've been all night, I've simply stopped keeping track of the money. When the texts from the guys come in, I answer them. That's all I can do. Try to keep up. I suppose I *could* have asked the guys to text me every time they win and in what amount, but, early on, once we became convinced the algorithm was working as hoped, Aiden suggested the guys keep payout information to themselves.

"The payouts will be what they'll be," he texted. "I'd rather agree to stop at a particular time and meet in the room to see where we're at. How does six am sound?" Everyone agreed that was a great idea. And that was that. I've been busier than a long-tailed cat in a room full of rocking chairs ever since, and I have no idea how much money the guys have amassed.

I take another guzzle of my coffee and clack on my keyboard again, but before I've penetrated The Venetian's backbone to find Aiden his next machine, my phone buzzes with an incoming text. It's Aiden, sending a message to the group text.

It's 6:00. Stop what you're doing.
Head to the room, fellas. See you in
about fifteen minutes, chicken girl.

I glance at the clock—it's six o'clock on the button—and then tap out a reply to Aiden.

Can't wait to find out the tallies!

A text from my father comes in.

On my way.

And then one from Aiden's father.

Playing one more slot. Been playing it for
ten minutes. Will play five more minutes
and then come up, whether it hits or not.

I put my phone on the desk, rise out of my chair, and stretch my arms above my head. What a night.

My phone buzzes on the desk. I glance down. It's from Aiden's father.

Slot just hit! Woohoo! Coming now. Fellas,
meet in the lobby of the Bellagio.
We'll go to the room together.

Roger that.

Roger.

I yawn again and amble to the floor to ceiling window overlooking the Strip. The sun is just coming up. The dawn of a new day. Behind me, I hear the sound of the door opening. I whirl around, just in time to see my nefarious crew burst into the room. The three men look exhausted but euphoric. And I'm right there with them. *What a night.*

I bound across the room and throw my arms around Aiden first. He squeezes me tightly and lays an exuberant kiss on my mouth. I move to Aiden's father, and he surprises me by picking me up off the floor and whooping with glee. Finally, I turn to my father and pause, suddenly feeling awkward. But when he opens his arms to me, my resolve to keep him at arm's length melts. I go to him and let him wrap his arms around me. Can I honestly say I forgive my father? No. But standing here in his arms, knowing he came here tonight and offered to help me, even at risk to himself, I'm sure of one thing: I still love him, despite his past sins.

When I pull out of my embrace with my father, I look at all three men expectantly. "Well?" I ask. "How'd we do?"

"Take it away, Raymond," Aiden says, ceding the floor to my father.

Smiling, Dad plops his burner phone onto the desk, followed by a stack of bills. "Fifteen thousand thirty-seven bucks."

"Wow," I say. "Great." But if I'm being honest, that total is slightly disappointing to me. I thought for sure we'd come closer to pocketing twenty-five grand tonight. "Aiden and I will definitely be able to—"

"That's just your dad's winnings," Aiden says. Without further ado, he plops his burner phone onto the desk, followed by a stack of bills. "Twenty-three thousand two hundred."

"What?" I blurt. "Oh, my God."

Aiden laughs. "I got lucky in my first fifteen casinos. Nobody on my machines and they all hit pay dirt in record time. So I figured why not start at the beginning and get through as many casinos as possible a second time around?" He taps his temple. "I'd noticed a shift change at three, so I knew nobody would remember me from the first go around. I figured I'd make hay while the sun was shining, as Gramps loved to say."

"I can't believe it," I say. "It was so chaotic and crazy up here, I didn't even realize you doubled back. I just assumed you'd hit a bunch of squatters and duds."

"Nope. That first round, I couldn't miss. It was like shooting fish in a barrel. I felt like the luckiest guy in the world."

"Amazing," I say. "How'd you do, Nick?"

Nick puts his bills onto the table, followed by his burner phone. "Seventeen grand and change." He winks at his son. "I noticed that shift change at three, too. I also went for a second round."

My heart is palpitating wildly. "You guys, that's over fifty-five grand here!"

For the next few minutes, we talk energetically with everyone sharing their experiences of the night.

"Hey, anyone else starving?" Aiden's father says. "Why don't we have this conversation over room service?"

We call downstairs to room service and order four large breakfasts, a huge pot of coffee, a carafe of orange juice, and a big bottle of champagne, and then we settle around the room to await the delivery of the food.

"That was the best night of my life," Aiden's father says, shaking his head. "It's every gambler's dream to hit jackpot after jackpot all night long. Man, what a rush."

"I must admit I've never had so much fun in my life," my father says. "I would have paid to get to do that."

We all laugh.

"It was amazing," Aiden says. He shoots me a huge smile. "Thank you, Savvy."

I wink.

When the food comes, we pour the champagne and raise our glasses.

"To algorithms," Aiden says. He salutes my father and me.

"And good-old-fashioned street smarts," I add, indicating Aiden and his dad.

Aiden's face turns earnest. "Thank you so much, everyone. Especially Savvy." His eyes are trained on mine. "I'm most definitely the luckiest guy in the world."

My heart skips a beat. I nod and smile, feeling too choked up to speak.

"Let's eat!" Aiden's father says, and we all laugh and dig into our food.

As we eat, we talk and laugh and marvel at the amazing night. Finally, when breakfast is done and everyone looks like they're about to tip over from sleep deprivation, my father hugs me and says he'll call me in a few days to check in...if that's okay with me.

"Sounds good," I say.

His face flushes. "I love you, honey."

I pause, my heart clanging. "I love you, too."

Another hug, and off Dad goes, looking like he's going to break down and sob the minute he gets out of the room.

"I'd better head out, too," Aiden's dad says as the door closes behind my father. "Thanks for letting me join the party. It felt so good to help Aidy get his guitar back. And on top of that, I got to bilk the casinos for a little bit of the money they've taken from me over the years, too. Ha! Heaven." He hugs me. "You're a living doll, Savvy baby. I'll see you in LA, right?"

"You sure will," Aiden says, and I physically swoon.

Aiden's father turns to leave but I stop him. "Hold on, Nick. After Aiden's twenty-five grand, there's almost thirty-one grand left in the pot. Let's split it between the two of us."

"Nah, keep it all for you and Aiden," Nick says. "Tonight wasn't about me. It was about me finally getting to help Aiden.

And on top of that, I got to have the time of my life tonight, too."

"Take some money," I insist. I grab a stack of bills and begin counting out fifteen grand.

"No, no," Nick says, gently pushing my hand away. "Tonight was my penance for all the times I've fucked Aidy over. He gave up two years of his life for me. Then his entire life savings and Betty. If you want to pay anyone anything, then pay Aiden."

"Take the money, Dad," Aiden says. "You've got Bethany and her kid to think about now, remember?"

Aiden's father looks torn. Clearly, the mention of Bethany and her son got him thinking. "Actually, yeah. Bethany's been talking about saving up for some fancy piece of equipment. Something to help her manufacture her jewelry faster so she can fill big orders. She said it costs about five grand."

"Perfect," I say, counting out the money. "Give a man a fish, he eats for a day. Give him the rod, he eats for a lifetime."

Aiden's father pauses.

"Take it," Aiden says.

Sighing, Nick takes the money from me. "Thank you. You're every bit as sweet as Aiden said you were."

"Oh, wow. Aiden said I'm sweet, did he?"

"No," Aiden says. "I told him you're the sweetest girl *ever*."

CHAPTER THIRTY

SAVANNAH

The minute the door shuts behind Aiden's father, Aiden and I rip our clothes off and begin mauling each other. As we kiss and grope, we tumble onto the bed, a frenzy of lips and fingers and warm breath. Aiden begins kissing my body—my stomach and hips and pelvis. My inner thighs. And I throw my head back and surrender to him completely—opening my legs and heart and very soul to him.

"Everything you touch turns to gold," he whispers as his lips kiss their way toward my aching tip. "You're my good luck charm."

Aaaaah.

His warm tongue finds my clit and begins swirling magically, making it throb and jolt and spasm with pleasure. I grip the bedsheet. And then, as my pleasure ramps up, I move my grip to the top of Aiden's head. When bliss threatens to slam into me, I pull roughly on Aiden's hair and moan with pleasure.

"Oh, sweet Jesus," I coo softly when my body tightens sharply from deep inside, threatening to release. When Aiden doubles down on what he's doing, I press myself into his mouth, my pelvis riding his mouth in a rhythm that matches the voracious movements of his lips and tongue and fingers. "Aiden," I grit out. "*Yes.*" I claw at him, gasping and gripping his hair like a lifeline. I moan and buck and whimper and writhe... and finally...*delicious.* In a flash of almost painful pleasure, my innermost muscles seize sharply, and then twist and warp around Aiden's magical tongue and fingers. In short, I come undone.

When Aiden emerges from between my thighs, his face is flushed. His eyes are blazing. His lips are shiny. He looks voracious. Drunk on arousal. *Beautiful.*

In record speed, he grabs a foil packet, gets himself covered, and crawls on top of me like a panther. He plunges himself inside me and burrows deep, deep, deep, growling like a wild animal. And I'm right there with him. In this moment, I don't feel human. I feel wild and unleashed.

I hike my thighs up around Aiden's ribcage and grip his ass and revel in the sensation of his warm, muscled body moving ferociously on top of mine.

"You feel so good," Aiden murmurs into my ear. He kisses my neck as his body dominates mine. "You're magic, Savvy. Pure magic." Without warning, he flips me over and sinks into me from behind. "I can't get enough of you," he growls into my ear, his body pounding into mine, his fingers working my clit. "I'm addicted to you. I'm fucking addicted."

I'm suddenly in complete overload. Every cell in my body, every molecule, every atom, surges, all at once, and then releases in an orgasm that sends me jolting like a fish on a line.

Aiden comes behind me, his moans of pleasure utterly

electrifying to me. And when our bodies quiet down, Aiden slides off me and pulls me close. For several minutes, we lie quietly in the day's first glow of sunlight, our chests heaving, our bodies spooned.

His skin is warm. His arms are wrapped around me. My eyelids are beginning to flutter and droop as I survey the sun beginning to peek out over the Strip.

"Chicken girl?" Aiden whispers.

"Hmm?" I reply, on the cusp of slipping under.

"I don't want to be with anyone else. I only want to be with you."

I smile sleepily. "I don't want to be with anyone else, either."

"Exclusive, then?"

"Absolutely."

He takes a deep breath behind me and says his next words on his exhale. "Holy fuck, I'm a lucky bastard."

I sigh happily. "Good night."

"Good night, little chicken. Amazing job tonight. This morning. Whatever. You kicked serious ass."

I mumble something meant to be, "Thank you."

"I'm in awe of you, Savvy. Completely blown away."

They're the last words I hear before I fall into blissful sleep.

CHAPTER THIRTY-ONE

SAVANNAH

Saturday, 4:23 p.m.

My stomach growls, and my eyes flutter open. The shower is running in the bathroom. Aiden's side of the bed is empty. I slide out of bed and head into the bathroom and discover Aiden standing naked in the clear Plexiglas shower, looking like a wet dream. His eyes are closed. Water is pelting the top of his head. Plumes of steam are rising up around his perfect, hard, muscled body. He looks like a fantasy. A Greek god. I stand, gawking at him for a long moment—salivating at the way the soapy suds drift down his sleek skin and traverse every nook and cranny of his cut abs and then slide down the full length of his penis. Holy crap, that man definitely has a prison body. And that face! His face is even more beautiful to me now than when I first met him—now that I know his perfect, symmetrical features are nothing but a brochure for his beautiful heart.

When Aiden finishes rinsing his hair, he opens his startling blue eyes and discovers me staring at him from the doorway. A slow, sexy smile spreads across his handsome face. "Join me," he says simply.

I don't need to be asked twice.

When I enter the shower, Aiden reaches for me to kiss me, but I've got a different idea. Wordlessly, I kneel before him and, as hot water rains down on me, take his full length into my greedy mouth.

As his dick thickens in my mouth, Aiden exhales and runs his fingertips across my wet head. A minute later, as I get into a rhythm, he grabs fistfuls of my wet hair and begins gyrating into my mouth. When he moans loudly, excitement surges inside me. I begin touching myself with one hand while gripping the base of his shaft with the other.

When an orgasm grips me, I disengage from him with a loud pop, too overcome with pleasure to do anything but close my eyes and moan.

Even before I've finished climaxing, Aiden yanks me to standing and roughly turns me around. As hot water rains down on us, he pins me against the Plexiglas wall of the shower and spreads my legs roughly like he's frisking me. I lay my palms flush against the slick surface, my body twitching and jolting with anticipation, my crotch throbbing with yearning.

As hot water cascades down my back, Aiden kneels down behind me and begins devouring every square inch of me. It's something no man has ever done to me before—at least, not like this. With such a lack of inhibition. Such *abandon*. And the sensation of his tongue and lips and teeth in forbidden places sends me into complete overload. I come hard.

When my climax ends, Aiden rises and presses his lips against my ear. "I want to fuck you without a condom. I'm clean. I'll pull out."

"I'm on the pill," I gasp out, hot water battering me. "Fuck me hard."

With a loud groan, Aiden reaches between my legs to find his target and then plunges into me with breathtaking fervor. My palms resting on the Plexiglas of the shower for support, I spread my legs and take what he's giving me. And what he's giving me is beastly. Not gentle in the slightest. *And I love it.* When I come after a few minutes of getting pounded, it's from muscles at my deepest core.

"Savvy," Aiden blurts behind me as his body ripples and jolts. He presses his hard body against my back. "What are you doing to me?" He turns me around and cups my face in his palms and kisses me as hot water rains down on us. "I can't believe what you did for me."

We finish washing and dry off with fluffy white towels and then move into the room to get dressed.

"It blows my mind I only met you three days ago," I say, rummaging through my small suitcase. "It feels like I've known you forever."

"Well, how long does a typical date last in the real world? Three hours?"

"I have no idea," I say. "I don't think I've ever been on a 'typical' date. Not the way they show them in the movies, anyway."

"Neither have I. But don't normal people go out to dinner and a movie or something?"

"I think so. I don't know."

"Okay, my point is that we've spent so much time together these past three days, we've probably had the equivalent of ten or fifteen dates in the real world. You know, for normal people."

"Who are these normal people going on dates?" I ask.

"I don't know. You're missing my point. I'm saying normal people go out on dates. And they don't see each other every day when they're first dating. They see each other maybe three times per week, I'd think. Maybe? So you could say we've been together the *equivalent* of five weeks."

I chuckle.

"You've heard of dog years, right?" he says. "Well, we've had chicken years. We've been dating five weeks in chicken."

I giggle. "Okay. Works for me."

Aiden looks at the clock. "Hey, what time does the reunion start? You want to grab a bite beforehand or afterwards?"

I slide on my underwear. "I don't care about going to the reunion. Let's take five hundred bucks from our winnings and treat ourselves to a five-star meal and a show."

Aiden shakes his head. "Hell no. We're going to that reunion."

"Why?" I say. "I couldn't care less what Mason Crenshaw thinks about me."

Aiden laughs. "We're not going to the reunion for you. We're going for *me*."

CHAPTER THIRTY-TWO

AIDEN

I zip up the back of Savvy's dress. "Sexy dress. Turn around. I want to get a good look at your hotness."

Savvy complies, gracing me with a smile that stops my heart.

"You look incredible," I say. And it's the truth. She's wearing a red dress that hugs her ample curves perfectly and sets off her shiny, dark hair.

"You look smokin' hot yourself," she says. "I love the shirt. Is that the one you bought when I was working on the algorithm?"

"Yeah, I ducked into a shop on the Strip right before I went to the storage room."

"Oh, yeah. That reminds me. When can I hear the song you wrote?"

A flock of butterflies releases into my stomach. *Shit.* I haven't written a song about a real girl since I was a teenager. Usually, when I write a song that could be classified as a "love song," it's about a fantasy girl. A perfect girl I make up in my head who couldn't possibly exist in real life.

Savvy cocks her head to the side, apparently seeing

something intriguing on my face. "What's the song about?"

I swallow hard. "You."

"*Me?* Oh, my gosh. When can I hear it?"

"The thing is, I don't normally write songs on piano. I prefer writing on guitar. Why don't I play it for you when we get to LA?"

"You truly think I'm going to wait that long to hear this song? Hell no. I want to hear that song right now."

"Savvy, no. Seriously. I can't sing it for you *now*."

"But you wrote it on piano. I'm sure it sounds great."

I pause. *Shit*. "At least let me get myself a little liquid courage before I play it for you."

"Why? You're an amazing musician. A professional. You play every week in front of strangers."

"I'm not doubting my musicianship or songwriting skills. I'm nervous to play it for you because..." I feel my cheeks turning red. "Because the song is really personal."

"Oh."

I glance away from Savvy's glowing face toward the big pile of cash sitting on the table. "We'd better put that money in the safe in the closet before we head out. A maid might come in, even if we put the Do Not Disturb sign on the door." I stride over to the money and begin gathering it, my heart racing. "Are you hungry? You want to grab food before the reunion or after?"

She joins me at the little table. "Will you promise to play the song after the reunion?"

I bite my lip. "Okay."

"Then let's go to the reunion now," she says, grabbing her

little purse off the bed. "We'll go to the reunion, hit the storage room, get a fancy dinner, and then see a late-night show. Sound like a plan?"

"Sounds amazing."

"Cool. How much of the cash should we spend on dinner and a show? What's our budget?"

"It's up to you," I say. "This money is yours."

Savvy and I begin walking toward the safe in the closet.

"No, the money is *ours*," she says. "After we take the money for Betty off the top, the rest we'll split fifty-fifty."

"I'm getting what I need to buy back Betty. That's all I could ever ask for."

"But you need money to live on, Aiden. You wired your life's savings to save your father."

I sigh. She's right. The truth is I desperately need money. But so does Savvy. "Yeah, but you lost your job," I say. "You've got a condo."

"I've already received four emails from recruiters asking me to interview for positions next week. I'm sure I'll have a new job soon."

"Wow. That's awesome. Congratulations. But I'm not gonna take a handout from you. That money is yours. You earned it. I did nothing."

She sighs. "Well, will you work for money, then?"

I shoot her a snarky look. "Babe, don't even joke about that. My body isn't for sale."

Savvy giggles. "No, no. I've got a legitimate offer of employment. How about I take ten grand for myself—just in case a new job doesn't materialize as fast as I think it will. And with the rest, I'll pay you to help me renovate my condo. I'll even throw in an untrained, unskilled laborer you can boss around during the renovation."

"You're serious?"

"Absolutely. I have a fixer-upper condo needing renovation. You work construction. Do you honestly think you could do a good job for me?"

Adrenaline floods me. "I know I could. I'd do an exceptional job for you."

"Great. You're hired."

"Do you want me to sign a written contract? I will."

Savvy rolls her eyes. "That won't be necessary. I trust you."

My heart leaps. "Okay. Thank you."

"And I'm in no rush to get the work done, by the way," Savvy says. "Just fit it in between music gigs. Oh, and you can stay at the condo overnight whenever you want, if doing that will make it easier to fit in gigs and work on the condo and have lots of sex with me." She grins.

I can't believe my ears. "You're sure about this?"

"Aiden, I can honestly say I've never been more sure about anything in my life."

Every molecule in my body electrifies. "Neither have I," I say.

"Good. It's settled, then. We're totally doing this. We're both all-in."

I nod. "We sure as fuck are. Awesome." I bite my lip. She's never looked more beautiful to me than she does in this moment. "Now let's go down to the bar, do some shots of tequila, and then head to the reunion. I want Mason Crenshaw to see the girl in the chicken suit grew up to become a swan."

CHAPTER THIRTY-THREE

SAVANNAH

As Aiden and I walk toward the entrance of the ballroom where the reunion is being held, my phone buzzes with an incoming text from Kyle.

Are you at the reunion yet?

> *Heading there literally right now. Thirty
> yards away from the front entrance.*

"Hey, I'm gonna hit the bathroom before we head in," Aiden says, indicating a restroom immediately to the right of the ballroom entrance.

"Okay. I'll wait here."

And off Aiden goes.

My phone buzzes again. I look down. It's Kyle again.

*Text me a secret photo of Mason C!
I want to see what he looks like now.*

*Only if I can do it without him
noticing. Wouldn't want him
thinking I actually give a fuck.*

I attach a barfing emoji to the end of my message, press send, and then quickly tap out a follow-up.

*Hey did you ever look at
those videos I sent you?*

What videos?

Aiden Jameson!

Who's that?

THE MUSICIAN!

*Oooooh. Shit. When you sent that text, I was at
a concert. Music too loud to watch the videos.
And then I totally forgot. Sorry. I'm at a concert
now, but I promise to watch when I get back to
my hotel room. Forgive me?*

*I'll forgive you if you promise
to watch the videos tonight!*

Promise.

I open my clutch to stuff my phone inside when it buzzes with another text from Kyle.

OMG! You fucked the musician, didn't you?

A huge smile on my face, I tap out a succinct reply.

Yes.

*How? When? You found Derek
with that woman on Wednesday!*

*Correct. And then I went to a bar
and got drunk and met Aiden and
had sex with him that night.*

NO FUCKING WAY!

*And it was the best sex of my life.
BY FAR. And then it turned into sooo
much more than sex. OMG, Kyle. I have
so much to tell you! I'll call you tomorrow
and tell you everything. In the meantime,
watch those damned videos!*

Okay. Gonna take a peek now.
Too loud to hear him, but now
I have to see this guy.

"You ready?"

I look up. It's Aiden.

"Yep." I hold up my phone. "I was just texting with Kyle. Remember? My next-door neighbor best friend who took me to the Halloween party in high school? He was supposed to come to the reunion tonight, but he had to cancel at the last minute."

My phone buzzes with an incoming text, and I look down.

Holy shit! He's hot AF! OMFG!
You fucked HIM? You're a
savage beast, Savage!

"Excuse me," I say calmly to Aiden, my cheeks flooding with heat. "Just need to finish up this conversation before we head inside."

"Take your time."

"Thanks."

I've been fucking him nonstop since
Wednesday! And I plan to continue
fucking him as much as humanly possible
for the foreseeable future. SO WATCH
THE DAMNED VIDEOS! You want
to discover amazing new music instead
of babysitting entitled rock stars? Well,
discover Aiden Jameson! PS He has zero

idea my best friend works for a record label. This is all my idea. He's not using me, if that's what you're thinking.

Wasn't thinking that at all.
You're gorgeous. Smart. Funny.
If anything, you're using him.
Duh. I'll watch the videos tonight.
Love you. Have fun!

Thanks! Love you, too!

I shove my phone into my little velvet clutch and smile at Aiden. "Thanks for waiting."

Aiden puts his arm out and I take it. "Come on, baby. Let's bring Mason Crenshaw to his knees."

CHAPTER THIRTY-FOUR

SAVANNAH

The moment Aiden and I cross the threshold into the reunion, every fiber of my body screams at me to turn around and run away. What the hell am I doing here? I've got nothing to prove to these people, least of all Mason Crenshaw. I'd much rather be sitting at some Cirque Du Soleil show with Aiden or walking along the Strip with him than putting on a show here. Actually, no. What I *really* want to be doing is sitting next to Aiden on a piano bench in a storage room, listening to him sing me that song he wrote about me. "Hang on," I say, stopping just inside the double doors of the ballroom. "I think I'm having a panic attack."

Aiden stops alongside me, his brow furrowed with concern.

"Let's leave," I say. "I'd so much rather—"

"Welcome, Wildcat!" a female voice sings out to us.

Trembling, I turn toward the voice to find none other than the most popular girl from school, Amanda Silvestri, walking toward us. She's wearing a sparkly silver dress, sky-high heels, and a wide smile. And, man, she looks even more stunning than she did back in high school.

"Be sure to grab your nametags off the table!" Amanda says gaily, her blue eyes shifting from Aiden to me without a hint of recognition in them. Clearly, the girl doesn't recognize me, which means she has no idea if it's Aiden or me who's the returning Wildcat. And I'm not surprised about that. I look quite a bit different than I did five years ago when I stood in front of my graduating class and gave the Valedictory speech. Plus, I'm guessing Amanda only became aware of my existence that very day—and that's assuming she stayed awake through any portion of my speech. And I don't blame her. Why would Amanda have known about me? For four years, she'd been busy doing whatever prom queens and class presidents do while I'd been busy hanging out with the nerd brigade and competing in mathalons. To put it mildly, our paths didn't cross.

I put out my hand. "Hi, Amanda. I'm Savannah Valentine. You probably don't remember me, but I'm—"

"*Savvy?*" Amanda bellows. She ignores my extended hand and throws her arms around me like we're long lost friends. "I didn't even recognize you! You look *gorgeous*." She giggles happily and disengages from me, her smile at full wattage. "*I probably don't remember you?* Savvy, you were the smartest person in school. And so witty and funny and pretty, too! I was always in awe of you!"

Come again? "Wow," I say lamely, my cheeks flushing. "Thank you. I was always in awe of *you*. You were always so poised and beautiful and full of life."

Amanda puts her hand on her chest. "Aw, thank you. So how are you?"

"Well, let's see. I lost my dream job three days ago, so that sucks. But I can honestly say I've never been happier in my life." I shoot Aiden a smile that tells him he's the reason for my present state of joy. "Speaking of which, let me introduce my... Aiden." I press my lips together. Crap. I was about to call Aiden my boyfriend. But, suddenly, I'm not sure if our agreement to be *exclusive* necessarily means we're going to call each other—

"I'm her boyfriend," Aiden says, extending his hand to Amanda. "Nice to meet you."

Amanda looks at me while shaking Aiden's hand, her face aglow. "I'm sorry to hear you lost your dream job, Savvy." She indicates Aiden. "But I can't imagine anything could bring you down when you've got this guy standing by to comfort you."

I giggle. "True."

"Savvy's gonna be just fine," Aiden says. "She's already got recruiters trying to scoop her up. The girl is a genius."

"Oh, I know. Everyone in the school knew Savvy would grow up to do remarkable things." Amanda flashes me a smile that's so warm and genuine, I suddenly feel like a moron for making Mason Crenshaw the centerpiece of my reunion fantasies. Why didn't I want to come here simply to connect with nice people like Amanda? People I might have missed out on in high school because I was too insecure to think they'd want to be friends with me?

"So how long have you two been together?" Amanda asks.

My heart stops. *Shit.* "Uh, actually, we—"

"Have been together five weeks," Aiden says. "We met in a bar, and that was it for both of us. We both felt like we'd been hit by a lightning bolt, and we've been inseparable ever since."

Amanda visibly swoons. "Oh, my gosh. You two are

hashtag relationship goals." She motions to Aiden's tattoos. "Are you a musician, Aiden?"

He nods. "I'm not selling out arenas by any stretch, but I'm a working musician in LA with regular gigs, and that's good enough for me."

"Aiden's being modest," I say. "He's absolutely brilliant. Check out Aiden Jameson on YouTube, and get ready to lose your mind. I promise you'll never be the same again after you've heard Aiden sing one of his songs. He's amazing."

Aiden blushes. "Thank you."

The three of us talk for a few more minutes about Aiden's music. And then about my nascent idea to try my hand at freelance cybersecurity work. Amanda tells us about her job as a first-grade teacher for a bit, and then Aiden and I say our goodbyes to Amanda and enter the reunion.

"I thought you said you didn't have any 'cool kid' friends in high school," Aiden says as we walk, hand in hand, into the heart of the crowded ballroom. "Amanda sure seemed to think you two were besties."

"She did, didn't she?" I say. "I don't really know what to say. I think maybe I created electric fences for myself in high school that just weren't there." We stop walking in the thick of the room and survey the crowded ballroom. I gasp and turn away from the entrance. "*He's here.*"

Aiden looks around. "Where?"

"The entrance. He just walked in."

Aiden's gaze snaps toward the double doors. "There's a bunch of guys coming in together. Which one is Mason?"

Oh, God, I can't bring myself to look toward the door. I'm

shaking. "Brown hair. Fit body. Dark shirt. Look for the guy whose face looks so cocky, you feel the uncontrollable urge to punch him in the teeth."

Aiden's eyes narrow as he continues staring toward the double doors...and then visibly ignite. "Hello, Mason." He takes a step to his left, making it seem like he's engaged in deep conversation with me, when, actually, he's staring over my shoulder toward Mason. "Come to papa, motherfucker."

"Can you tell if he's here with a date?" I whisper.

"No, he's stag. He's surrounded by a bunch of big dudes. He was the quarterback?"

"Yeah. He got a full ride to UNLV. He did okay there. Nothing spectacular. I heard he's in sales for a fertilizer company now."

Aiden juts his chin. "I'm guessing those big guys around him were his offensive line in high school." He scoffs. "What a cliché." Aiden silently stares over my shoulder for a long moment, his eyes blazing. "I'm sure he came stag figuring he'd leave with some 'lucky' girl tonight." He stares for another beat. "Amanda is chatting him up. Okay, now he's looking around the room, scoping things out. Oh, he's heading into the party." Without warning, Aiden waves enthusiastically in the direction of the double doors. "Hey, Mason! Hey!"

"What are you doing?" I whisper.

"Calling to my good buddy, Mason Crenshaw." He waves again, this time even more enthusiastically. "Hey, Mason!"

"Stop!" I whisper urgently. "I wanted it to happen organically. *Casually.*"

"Too late for that. He's coming over here." Aiden smiles

like an assassin and calls out, "Hey, Mason! Great to see you!"

Mason comes to a stop right next to me, but I keep my head down and stare at his shoes.

"Hey," Mason says. "I'm sorry. Do I...? I don't think I remember you, man."

"No, you wouldn't. We've never met before. I'm just a plus-one tonight. Here with my girlfriend. I think you know her. *Savvy Valentine.*"

There's a beat of thick silence.

"Savvy?" Mason finally whispers.

My blood thumping in my ears, I look up to find Mason staring at me, his jaw hanging open.

"Hi," I say. But that's all I can muster.

Aiden leans forward. "Savvy told me about what happened at the Halloween party. You know, how you took her virginity in a closet and then came to school the next Monday and told her she was nothing but a pity-fuck?"

Oh, shit. Aiden's voice could cut steel.

Aiden takes a menacing step forward, his chest heaving and his jaw clenched. "You knew it was Savvy's first time, man. You knew she had a crush on you. And you didn't even try to make it special for her. Didn't even try to make it nice. You told her she was a charity case, when, in reality, she was slumming with you. So I think you owe her an apology, don't you?"

My chest squeezes. I've never seen Aiden like this. He suddenly looks exactly like what he is...a felon. A man who carved his spectacular body behind iron bars.

Mason turns his gaze on me. "Wow, Savvy. You've been so obsessed with me for five years, you felt the need to bring this thug here to—"

Gah. Before I can process what's happening, Aiden is lurching forward and grabbing a fistful of Mason's shirt. Mason responds by pushing hard on Aiden's chest. And, suddenly, the two men are going at it.

And what am I doing? Wigging out. Not keeping my cool in the slightest.

The scuffle doesn't last long, though. In a flash, Mason's friends appear out of nowhere and leap to Mason's defense. They grab Aiden and hold him back. And that prompts a couple random dudes standing nearby to hold Mason back, thankfully. And then, for a confusing, harrowing moment, both men scream at each other at the tops of their lungs.

"Okay, everyone just—" I begin to say...but I'm interrupted by a familiar male voice shouting my name to my left. I turn my head and, oh, for the love of fuck, the voice belongs to none other than *Derek. Son of a bitch!* He's sprinting toward Aiden at full speed, his right hand balled into a tight fist and cocked as he shouts about Aiden's guitar tattoo and tells everyone Aiden is a rapist who roofied me. "No!" I scream. But my words have no impact whatsoever. Derek reaches Aiden, who's still immobilized by Mason's posse, and lands a vicious punch to Aiden's jaw.

Screaming, I fling myself toward Derek like a missile, and push on his shoulder with all my might, desperately trying to protect Aiden from taking another hit while he's being held back. And the next thing I know, I'm stumbling backward and crashing hard to the floor. What the hell just happened? It takes a half second for me to realize Derek just swatted me away like King Kong on top of the Empire State Building. *He pushed me to the floor!* And so forcefully, he knocked the wind out of me.

I look up from the ground, shocked, to find Mason grabbing ahold of Derek, keeping him from pummeling Aiden.

"Let him go!" Mason yells to his friends, and they release Aiden, just as Derek breaks free of Mason and takes a swing, landing a punch to Mason's cheek.

But now that Aiden is free, he comes flying at Derek like a missile, dropping him to the ground. In a flash, Aiden begins beating the shit out of Derek as Mason and his friends shout their approval.

"Aiden!" I scream. "Stop!" I leap up and shriek at Aiden, and, much to my relief, he somehow gets ahold of himself and stops wailing on Derek. But before getting off Derek for good, he pinches Derek's chin between his thumb and fingers and growls into his face, "If I killed you, you'd deserve it for hurting her, you piece of shit."

"Get that asshole out of here!" Amanda shouts...and, much to my relief, she's clearly talking about Derek, not Aiden. Aiden gets off Derek and steps aside, and a couple of Mason's large friends scoop Derek off the ground and literally drag him out the double doors.

Aiden lurches over to me, his face on fire. "Are you okay? Did he hurt you?"

"I'm fine. Freaked out, but fine."

Aiden touches my cheek gently. "You're sure?"

"I'm fine. What about you? Derek landed a nasty punch when Mason's friends were holding you back."

"I'm fine. He punches like a pussy. He wouldn't last a day in prison." He smirks.

I glance over Aiden's shoulder. Mason is standing in a large group, holding court. "Let's get out of here," I say. "If someone has called the cops, I don't want you anywhere near here. God knows what someone might say about you—and who they'll believe."

"Yeah, good thinking." Aiden takes my hand, and we begin moving swiftly toward the double doors. "Sorry I lost my shit. I'm not normally such a hothead. I was just—"

"Hey!" Mason's voice calls out. "Hold up!"

Crap. I glance in the direction of the voice, my stomach clenching, and, to my surprise, Mason is heading toward us with Amanda in tow...and the look on his face tells me he's most definitely coming in peace.

"Be nice," I whisper to Aiden. "Please, Aiden."

"He's not coming over to fight," he whispers. "He's coming over to apologize. As he should."

Mason and Amanda arrive.

"Are you okay, Savvy?" Amanda asks.

"I'm fine. Thank you. I was more shocked than hurt."

"Who was that guy?" she asks.

"My ex-boyfriend. It didn't end well."

Amanda looks at Aiden. "I'm glad you beat him up. He deserved it for pushing Savvy like that."

"Damn straight," Mason agrees.

"Yeah, hey, thanks for the backup," Aiden says to Mason. "That was unexpected."

"He pushed Savvy. Not cool." Mason looks at me and

grimaces. "I'm sorry, Savvy. For, you know, what happened in high school." He looks at Aiden. "I should have apologized to you out of the gate. I was just..."

"Swinging your dick," Aiden says. "But I was doing a bit of that myself. I probably shouldn't have come at you quite so hard right out of the gate."

"I'm sure I would have done the same thing if she'd been my girl."

Aiden nods at Mason and the two men visibly enter into a nonverbal truce. Now Aiden directs his smoldering gaze at me. "You ready to get out of here, chicken girl? I think I've outworn my welcome."

All four of us chuckle.

I hug Amanda. Wave goodbye awkwardly to Mason. And then take Aiden's hand as we walk toward the double doors. "Jesus, Aiden," I whisper as we exit the ballroom. "Please tell me you don't run around throwing punches on a regular basis."

Aiden chuckles. "I don't. Not saying it'll never happen again. But I'm not easily provoked, typically. It's awfully hard to play a guitar with swollen fingers. But I'm not gonna let anybody disrespect you, Savvy. Not verbally, and certainly not physically. I'll break both hands before I let anyone lay a pinky on you."

My entire body jolts with desire. I probably shouldn't be swooning at the primal edge in Aiden's voice, but I am. Yes, what happened in there was scary. Yes, it was probably stupid, too. But there's no denying a piece of me enjoyed watching Aiden leap to my defense like that. A primal part of me I didn't know existed before tonight.

When we pass through the doors of the ballroom, we see Derek sitting in an armchair at a far end of the large entrance lobby. He's got his head in his hands. His body language is utterly defeated.

"I need to talk to him," I say.

Aiden holds my arm. "No."

"Yes. I need to tell him you didn't drug me or coerce me in any way to make those videos. If I don't convince him of that—if he leaves here thinking I've been kidnapped or taken hostage by some rapist who roofied me— God only knows what he might do next."

"I'll go with you. I'm not letting you near him on your own."

"No. You two can't be together. Don't worry. He's not going to hurt me. He's just sitting there. I'm going to talk to him for two minutes and leave."

Aiden motions to a marble wall a few feet from where Derek is sitting. "I'll stand behind there. That way, I'll be able to overhear your conversation with him and protect you, if needed."

"Fine."

We approach Derek. Aiden gets himself situated behind the wall while I take the armchair next to Derek.

"Hey, Derek," I say softly.

He lowers his hands and looks up. His eyes are glistening. He's got a doozy of a contusion on his chin. A shiner that's swelling like crazy. "I didn't mean to push you," he says. "I've never once in my life touched a woman like that. I'm so sorry, Savvy. Are you hurt?"

"I'm fine," I say. "I just wanted to let you know Aiden isn't my captor. He didn't brainwash me or drug me or hurt me in any way. He's my *boyfriend*. I've been having consensual sex with him since Wednesday night. I met him and went for it because he's sexy as hell and I wanted him. It was as simple as that. I sent those videos to you on Wednesday night *by choice* because seeing you with that woman was humiliating and horrifying. I wanted to get back at you. In retrospect, I wish I hadn't sent those videos to you, not because I'm embarrassed that I'm with Aiden in them, but because I truly don't care enough about you to try to make you jealous."

Derek sighs. "You might *think* you had consensual sex with that guy, but he obviously took advantage of you that night, Savvy."

"Oh, you want to talk about a guy taking advantage of a woman!" I shout, suddenly enraged. "Do the words 'I love you' ring a bell, asshole?"

He looks shocked. "I *do* love you. Why do you think I'm here?"

I'm floored. "You love me?"

He nods. "Fucking someone else doesn't change the way I feel about you. Sex is just sex."

I put up my hands. "Oh, my God. Stop talking. Please." I sigh. "Why did you come here? You can't possibly want me. And I sure as hell don't want you."

"I truly thought you were in danger. You looked like you were having a psychotic breakdown at the top of that mountain on Wednesday. And then I got those videos, and I knew he had to have—"

"*He didn't.* Aiden hasn't done anything but treat me with respect since the minute he met me. You're the one who lied to my face to get into my pants and then physically assaulted me at my freaking high school reunion! Nice way to treat a woman you supposedly 'love.'"

"I'm sorry I pushed you. It was an accident. And I do love you. Just not *exclusively.*"

I stand. "Okay, we're done here. I don't know why I'm wasting my precious time talking to you when I could be with a man who actually cares about me. A man who respects me. A man of actual *integrity.*"

"*Integrity?* Did you forget you told me he's a *felon*? News flash, Savvy: they don't put men of *integrity* behind bars."

I lean forward sharply. "You don't know the first thing about Aiden. What he's been through in his life. The challenges he's faced. The hard choices he's had to make. You don't know what he's had to do to survive and try to find beauty and happiness in his life. How hard he's had to fight to make the right choices. So don't you dare for a minute judge him. You might throw around the word 'love' like Skittles at a toddler's birthday party, but Aiden knows the true meaning of that word. He puts everything on the line for the people he loves—*no matter what.* Because he's a man of action, not empty words. He's a man of true character." I flip him off with both hands. "So fuck you, Derek! Aiden's got more integrity in his pinky than you've got in your entire body!" I turn on my heel to march away, but on a sudden impulse, whirl around again. "Oh, and one more thing? Now that I've been with Aiden, I now know for a fact you're an absolutely horrible lay." With that,

I turn around and march away, straight around the corner... where I'm instantly met with the crush of Aiden's hungry lips.

CHAPTER THIRTY-FIVE

AIDEN

Savvy and I sprint hand in hand toward the elevator bank on the far side of the casino. "That was incredible," I say when we've reached the middle of the casino floor, and it's clear Derek isn't following us. "You were incredible back there. You were savage."

Savvy laughs. "That's Kyle's nickname for me! *Savage.*"

"He's exactly right. Oh, my God." I stop and pull her to me and kiss the hell out of her. "You're a savage beast, Savvy Valentine. Holy shit. You've never been sexier to me than right this minute."

Savvy giggles. "I feel incredible right now. On fire."

"Do you really believe all those things you said about me?"

"Every word."

Emotion grips me. "Are you sure? I'm the guy who had to leave after a scuffle because the cops might come and not believe a word I say. You sure you're okay with having a boyfriend like that?"

Savvy's expression surprises me. She doesn't look compassionate or sympathetic. She looks *pissed.* "If you don't want to be with me, then don't try to get *me* to break it off, okay? Just say it, Aiden. Say whatever you're really thinking."

"What? *No*." I clutch her shoulders. "Savvy, listen to me. I'm absolutely crazy about you. I'm just worried you're gonna look at me any day now and think, 'I can't be with *him*.'"

She looks up at the ceiling for a moment like she's asking God himself for patience, and when she looks at me again, her dark eyes are steely. "Do you want me? Yes or no."

"Yes. It scares me how much I want you."

"Great. That's all you need to worry about. What you want. You're in charge of your feelings. I'm in charge of mine. You want me. I want you. We stay together until any of those things changes for either of us." She clenches her jaw. "Okay?"

Warmth spreads throughout my core. I nod. "Okay."

"You don't get to tell me I shouldn't want to be with you. Or that you're not good enough for me. I'm in charge of my feelings and that's that. Same for you. Do we have a deal?"

"Yes. Absolutely. Holy shit, you're hot."

"Now take me to the bar for a fuckload of tequila shots, and then we're going to the storage room, and you're going to play me that motherfucking song."

I bite my lip and put out my arm. "Let's go."

CHAPTER THIRTY-SIX

I pull out a piece of paper from my pocket, unfold it, and place it on the piano in front of me. "I haven't memorized my lyrics yet," I explain sheepishly.

"This isn't *American Idol*," Savvy says. "I promise I won't judge you. I just want to hear what was going through your mind while I was upstairs slaving away on the algorithm."

"And, also, keep in mind piano isn't my primary instrument," I say. "When we get to LA, I'll play this song for you on my guitar, and it'll be *way* better."

"*Aiden*," Savvy says. "I know you only wrote this song yesterday. I know it's a first draft. I just want to hear the gist."

I take a deep breath and begin playing the song. I play a few simple chords to set the stage. Nothing too fancy. On piano, I'm not capable of playing anything too fancy. A few more simple chords and I begin to sing.

I needed a ride, and there she was
It was nothing more than that
She told me her secrets, I told her mine,
Tried, but I couldn't hold back

I'm Savvy, she said, but only by name
I told her I'd tell her goodbye
She said that's fine and flashed me a smile
That made me forget how to lie
And now she's...my...valentine
My...beautiful...
Savvy Who Isn't Savvy
And I'm Her Aiden Not Saying Goodbye
She's my Savvy Who Isn't Savvy
Won't stop 'til I've made her mine
I needed to save the one I love
Nothing more to it than that
But she gave me her heart so I gave her mine
Tried, but I couldn't hold back
Thought I knew what I wanted
At least, what I needed,
Turns out, didn't have a clue
No strings or frets worth a shit to me now
If Savvy's not here with me, too
Because she's...my...valentine
My...beautiful...
Savvy Who Isn't Savvy
One look sets my soul on fire
My Savvy Who Isn't Savvy
Won't rest 'til I've made her mine
She's Savvy Who Isn't Savvy
Sent straight from heaven above
She's my Savvy Who Isn't Savvy
And I'm Her Aiden Who's Fallen,
Her Aiden Who's Fallen,
Her Aiden Who's Fallen in Love

I lift my fingers off the piano keys, turn to smile at Savvy... and I'm met with her glorious lips on mine.

CHAPTER THIRTY-SEVEN

AIDEN

If I thought Savvy and I would come upstairs and "make love" after the sentiments I expressed to her in my song, I was happily mistaken. We're unleashed. Holding nothing back. Animals in a frenzy. And I love it.

With a loud groan, I lift Savvy up onto my cock and slam her back into the wall of the hotel room. She wraps her thighs around my waist while fucking me hard. I grab her ass with both hands and thrust myself deep inside her again and again, kissing her voraciously. But I can't get deep enough. Can't fuck her hard enough. I walk over to the bed with her clinging to me, guide her down, and bend her over the bed. I run my palm up and down her spine, teasing her, and finally grab her hair, pull her head back, and plunge myself inside her. When she cries out, I spank her ass, and she growls. When I reach around and massage her swollen tip, still pounding her, she whimpers and moans and growls. Another spank of her round ass and she comes for me. So hard, I feel wetness trickle down my balls.

I come inside her...so forcefully, my vision blurs and warps. And, suddenly, I know for a fact I'm not going anywhere. Ever. Because, for the first time in ten fucking years, I finally feel like I'm home.

CHAPTER THIRTY-EIGHT

SAVANNAH

The waitress refills my coffee mug, blocking my view of Aiden playing his acoustic guitar on the far side of the patio.

"Thank you," I say politely to the waitress, even though I feel like shrieking at her, "Move the fuck out of my way!"

"You're welcome," she says brightly, and then she's gone.

My gaze returns to Aiden. This isn't the first time I've watched him perform at his Sunday brunch gig, of course. It's the fourth time. Indeed, I've been here every Sunday since we got back from Vegas. Plus, I've watched Aiden play with various bands at tiny clubs. I've seen him playing piano at a seedy lounge in Burbank twice. Oh, and I tagged along to watch him lay down some guitar tracks for an artist making an indie album on a shoestring budget. And each and every time I've watched Aiden making music in any context, on any instrument, I've fallen more and more madly in love with him.

Not that I needed to watch Aiden making music to fall deeply and desperately and madly in love with him. I would have done that, regardless—just from spending time with the man and getting to know him, inside and out.

Since Aiden and I got back from Vegas four weeks ago,

we've been inseparable. Joined at the hip. I'm not employed, after all, and neither is Aiden—not in any conventional sense. Which means we've been free to spend as much time together as we like. And that's translated to us being together pretty much all the time. Day and night. Do we have lots of sex? Yes, of course. But that's not all we do. Not at all.

Over the past four weeks, besides having sex with Aiden and watching him play at various gigs all over LA, I've also watched him renovate my kitchen and bathroom. Sometimes, I sit close by while Aiden works. I open my laptop and work on a project for one of my new freelance clients, glancing up occasionally at Aiden and his bare chest and arms while he works. Other times, I help Aiden when he needs an extra pair of hands. Still other times, we go for a jog or hike or to the grocery store or the beach.

On nights when Aiden doesn't have a gig, we snuggle into my bed and have sex and then watch movies or cheesy TV shows afterward. Our obsession at the moment? *Magnum, P.I.* When we happened upon that cheesy show while channel surfing one night, I blurted, "That's the one the bartender told me about!" So, of course, I demanded we watch an episode... and now it's our favorite thing. *Is Higgins really Robin Masters?* We've simply got to know.

The crowd around me on the patio applauds, drawing me out of my thoughts.

"Thanks," Aiden says into his microphone. And then he launches into a John Mayer song called "Say."

As Aiden begins singing, my phone on the table vibrates with a text from Kyle.

Sorry I'm late. Are you there yet?

Yes. I got a table on the patio.
Back corner. No worries about being
late. I'm unemployed, remember?
I'm not in any rush.

See you in two minutes.

My stomach flips over with excitement. I can't wait to see my darling Kyle. It's been far too long. But, mostly, I'm excited for Kyle to meet Aiden. Or, rather, for Kyle to finally get to see my Aiden perform. When Kyle finally watched those videos of Aiden Jameson, he immediately called to gush. "I'd love to see him perform while I'm in LA," Kyle said. And now, finally, that's about to happen.

"Hey, Savage."

I look up. It's Kyle. Standing at the edge of my table. I pop up and give him a hug and kiss. "Hey, honey," I coo warmly. "So glad you could make it." I glance at Aiden playing and singing on the other side of the patio, and my heart squeezes at the expression of excitement on his face. Clearly, Aiden knows this is *it*. His big chance. Of course, I've told Aiden not to feel stress about today. "Kyle coming to see you isn't a make or break thing," I assured Aiden as we drove here together. "Just perform like you always do, and don't even think about Kyle watching you."

Yeah. Sure. Good luck with that. By the expression on

Aiden's face as he watches Kyle getting settled at our table, it's clear Aiden believes today's performance is, in fact, a "make or break" thing. And, frankly, if I'm being completely honest, I do, too.

"You look happy," Kyle says, picking up a menu.

I motion across the patio toward Aiden. "It's easy to feel happy with him in my life, especially while sitting here listening to him play."

Kyle's gaze follows my gesture. Aiden and Kyle lock eyes. Kyle waves. Aiden waves back as he continues singing. And I'm suddenly nervous as hell. *Please, God, let this be Aiden's lucky break.*

"Wow, great menu," Kyle says, his eyes scanning his choices.

"There's a reason for that long line outside," I say. "Everything is great here."

Applause rises up around us. Aiden has finished playing the John Mayer song.

"Thanks so much," Aiden says into his microphone. "This next song is really special to me. It's a song I wrote for my girlfriend, Savvy."

Kyle looks up from his menu and gives Aiden his full attention.

"I got really creative when I named this song about Savvy," Aiden continues. He pauses for effect. "It's called...'Savvy.'"

Everyone in the restaurant chuckles, including Kyle.

Aiden takes a deep breath and whispers. "This one's for you, baby." He strums the first chords of his now-familiar song, and my heart flutters with anticipation. Hearing this song never gets old, especially when Aiden plays it on guitar. I loved hearing Aiden play this song for me that first time on piano in the storage room. But since then, I've loved hearing him play it on guitar even more—both on his acoustic guitar, like he's playing today, and on Betty, his beloved Telecaster.

"He's even better in person than on those videos," Kyle says. "His charisma in person is unbelievable."

My heart lurches. "He's incredible, isn't he?" I say. "He's a star, Kyle. I'm sure of it."

Kyle watches Aiden quietly for a long moment. Finally, he smiles and says, "I've definitely got a good feeling about him, Savvy."

I bite my lip. "Really?"

Kyle nods. "I'd bet just about anything my boss will love him. I mean really, really love him."

"I know the feeling."

"I don't want my boss to see the videos, though. I want him to meet Aiden in person. That's gonna be key to sealing the deal."

Across the patio, Aiden barrels into singing the ending of his song, his blue eyes trained on mine like lasers.

She's my Savvy Who Isn't Savvy
And I'm so glad she's mine
She's my Savvy Who Isn't Savvy
And I'm her Aiden Till the End of Time

My lips part with surprise. Those are new lyrics. I flash Aiden a beaming smile, and he returns it.

He strums the last chord of his song, and the place erupts

in applause.

"I love you, Savvy," Aiden says into his microphone. "With all my heart. Thank you for loving me the way you do."

I sense every head in the restaurant turning to look at me—the lucky bitch he's talking to—but my eyes remain locked with Aiden's. I mouth my reply to him, exaggerating the movement of my lips to make sure my message is received loud and clear across the patio: *I love you, too. With. All. My. Heart.*

EPILOGUE

SAVANNAH

As I listen to Aiden performing from the wings of the massive stage, I can't help marveling that this is our life. What a year! The best year of my life.

About a week after Kyle saw Aiden perform at that brunch place in Silver Lake, he flew Aiden to New York City to meet his boss. Three weeks after that, Aiden inked a two-album deal with Kyle's record label. And a couple months after that, Aiden was in the studio recording his debut album—which, when released six months later, spawned *three* Billboard Top 100 hits, including Aiden's biggest hit. A little song called "Savvy."

And now, here we are, finishing up the US leg of a world tour. Specifically, for the past three months, Aiden has been the opening act for his idol, Lucas Ford, who, for the record, has turned out to be an awesome guy. Whatever problems Lucas might have had a year ago when Kyle was forced to babysit him in Denver, they're apparently fixed now. Probably thanks to his wonderful girlfriend—a spitfire with a blonde pixie cut who's become a close friend of mine these past three months on tour.

Oh, God, I've absolutely loved being on this tour. I've

been with Aiden. Made new friends. Seen new places. And the craziest part? I'm working and making money, too. Because when you're a freelance cybersecurity specialist, you can work anywhere, anytime, as long as you've got a laptop. Even while following your boyfriend around on his tour.

Aiden finishes his song on stage, and the crowd in the large arena roars its approval—and, of course, my body electrifies the same way it always does when a massive arena applauds my boyfriend's music. You'd think after months of watching humongous crowds go apeshit over Aiden, I'd become inured to the thrill of it all. But, nope. It still enthralls me, every single time.

"Thank you!" Aiden says into his microphone, and the crowd cheers again.

I can't see Aiden's face clearly, since I'm watching the show from the wings of the stage, and I'm positioned slightly behind Aiden and to the side. But I can tell from his voice and body language he's elated at this raucous crowd's reaction to him.

"So, hey," Aiden says to the audience. "Is anyone here excited to see Lucas Ford in just a bit?"

The crowd goes nuts.

"Yeah, me, too. That guy's been my idol since forever. I pinch myself every day I'm not only on tour with him, but I get to call him my friend."

The crowd cheers again.

"Hey, out of curiosity, before I leave and Lucas comes out here, would anyone be interested in hearing me play a song I wrote called 'Savvy'?"

The crowd goes bananas, the same way they always do at the mention of that particular song. It's Aiden's biggest hit, after all.

"All right. Let's do it, then." He turns to wink at me in the wings, and I flash him a beaming, goofy, effusive smile. And then he cues his band, readies his fingers across Betty's strings, and rips off the iconic, opening riff of his beloved hit.

As soon as Aiden begins singing, I feel an arm slide around my shoulder.

"Hey, Savvy."

I turn to find Lucas Ford's girlfriend squeezing me—the woman who's quickly become one of my best friends in the world. "Hey, girl," I reply. A quick squeeze back and I return to the show. I let my gaze drift over the faces in the crowd as they watch Aiden. And, of course, I sing along with the song. But, suddenly—weirdly—the words coming out of my mouth don't match Aiden's...*because he's changed the lyrics to the song.*

And now she's...my...valentine
My...beautiful...
Savvy Who Isn't Savvy
And I'm Her Aiden Not Saying Goodbye
She's my Savvy Who Isn't Savvy
Won't stop 'til I've made her my wife

My heart stops. Did Aiden just say...?

Aiden signals the band, and the music abruptly ceases. There's silence in the arena, other than the sound of blood thumping in my ears. The crowd titters in anticipation.

I hold my breath.

Aiden leans into his microphone. "Hey, do ya'll mind if I get Savvy Who Isn't Savvy out here for a sec? There's something I want to ask her."

The crowd goes nuts. But I'm frozen in place. A deer in headlights. Did he just say...?

Aiden turns toward the wings. "Savvy, baby? Could you come out here, sweetheart?"

I can't move. My legs won't function. *Oh, my God.*

Laughing, my friend squeezes my shoulders and guides me onto the stage. She deposits me in front of Aiden and glides away...and, yet again, the crowd loses its collective mind.

Aiden pulls his microphone out of its stand. "Savvy," he says softly. He grabs my hand with his free one. "You're the love of my life. My everything." He releases my hand in order to pull a ring box out of his jeans...and then he kneels, the ring box in his hand, a beautiful smile on his face, and says, "Savannah Valentine. Savvy Who Isn't Savvy. Savvy Whose Give-a-Shitter Done Broke. I love you with all my heart and soul. Will you please, *please* make me the happiest man alive and say yes to becoming my wife?"

Aiden opens the ring box to reveal a goddamned beast of a diamond, and I gasp.

"Yes," I choke out.

Laughing, tearing up, Aiden rises and wraps me in his muscled arms. He plants a huge kiss on my lips that makes me burst into tears. As the arena applauds and cheers, I throw myself into Aiden's arms. For a long moment, we hold on to each other, trembling with emotion.

"I love you," Aiden says into my ear. "I love you so much."

"I love you, too," I reply.

Wiping his eyes, Aiden disengages from me. He raises my hand into the air like I've just won a prize fight. "Ladies and gentlemen!" he booms into his microphone. "I give you my future wife...Savvy Who Isn't...*Single!*"

ALSO AVAILABLE FROM
WATERHOUSE PRESS

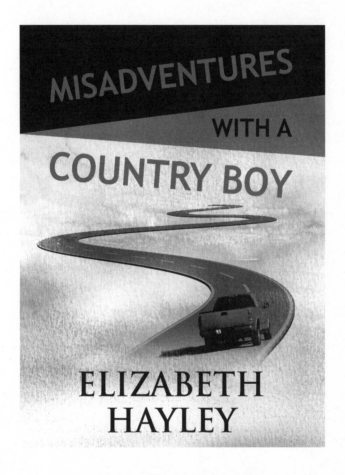

Keep reading for an excerpt!

EXCERPT FROM
MISADVENTURES WITH A COUNTRY BOY

"Hi. I'm Cole," he said, extending his hand. "You tell me your name, and then we won't be strangers anymore."

She remained silent and gave him a withering look.

"Fine." He shrugged. "If you're not gonna tell me your name, I'll pick one for you." Cole studied the girl from head to toe. She wore a gray T-shirt with a neck so wide it hung off one shoulder—the kind of T-shirt people paid a hundred dollars for. He would have gladly stretched out one of his shirts for a fraction of that price. She'd paired the overpriced shirt with tight blue jeans and black flats. The way she crossed her arms over her chest and impatiently tapped her foot reminded him of some of the girls from his hometown. Back home, a girl like her would have taken one look at a guy like him—his beat-up ride, dirt under his nails—and acted like a, well... "Let's go with Princess," Cole said, a faint smile on his lips.

She narrowed her eyes at him. "Not even close."

"What is it, then?"

Her gaze darted down to a twig beside her. She picked it up and tossed it a few feet away. "Rose," she said, though she didn't move to shake his hand. She looked him up and down, her expression making it clear she was still suspicious. "You're still a stranger."

Cole retracted his hand and slid it into his back pocket. "So tell me, then. How do I *stop* being a stranger?" Better judgment should have had him getting into his truck and driving away from this girl's drama. But his conscience wouldn't let him.

"You don't. You think just because we know each other's names that I should suddenly trust that you won't kill me later?"

Cole let out a loud laugh. She was funny...he'd give her that. But the name Rose was bullshit. The quirk of her lips and the way she averted her eyes told him she wasn't being honest. "You think I might kill you?"

She shrugged. "I don't know that you won't. Just because you have this whole...charming Southern thing going on"—she gestured up and down Cole's body with her hand—"doesn't mean you're not the next Ted Bundy."

"You think I'm charming?"

She rolled her eyes and huffed as if the question annoyed her. But Cole knew by the faint flush on her cheeks it hadn't. "I also said I think you might be the next Ted Bundy."

"I might also be Prince Charming."

Princess's expression softened, and the corners of her lips turned up slightly.

"Is that a smile?"

"No," she replied. Though he was certain she knew just as well as he did that it was.

"Listen, I'm honestly trying to help. You seem like you're trying to get someplace. But I understand if you don't want to take a ride from some dude you met at a gas station. If it'll make you feel better, you can text a picture of my license to a friend or somethin'." Cole reached into his wallet and removed his license for her to take.

She narrowed her eyes at him, as if deciding what to do next, before grabbing and studying his ID closely like she was looking for any information that would help make her decision clear.

"What are you looking for?" he asked.

"That doesn't really look like you." She unwrapped an orange Starburst from the pack she held in her hand and popped it into her mouth. She chewed slowly as she twisted the wrapper around her index finger.

"Well, it is. Same guy, different hair," Cole said, removing his hat to show her his hair. "Normally it's a little longer, like this."

She stood and leaned against the building, pressing one foot back on the dusty brick behind her. Tearing the Starburst pack open some more, she held it out to him.

"Thanks," he said, taking one.

Then she took out another orange one before shoving the pack into her bag and removing her phone. She turned it on and pressed a few buttons.

Cole gestured to the ancient flip phone she was holding. There was no way that was the one she normally carried with her. "Did you teleport here from 2002 or something?"

She stopped fidgeting with the buttons and glanced up

at him, her long black lashes framing her deep brown eyes perfectly. "Or something," she replied. Then she directed her attention back to the phone while Cole waited.

When she was done, she handed his license back to him and slid her phone back into the outside pocket of her backpack. "Okay, Cole Timmons from 116 North Washington Street, Samson, Georgia. I know where you live. And now so does my sister. So don't do anything crazy."

Cole raised his hands out to his sides innocently. "Wouldn't dream of it. Besides," he added, "I'm not the one with no ID who's carrying around a burner phone and eating only the *orange* Starbursts. If one of us is crazy, it's sure as hell not me."

She was silent for a moment before pushing off the wall and heading toward Cole's truck. And this time she didn't try to hide her smile.

Cole walked to the passenger side and stood in front of it, blocking his new companion from opening the door.

Her eyes shot to his. "What?"

"I have one condition for you ridin' with me."

She returned his glare, pulling her shoulders back and raising her eyebrows.

"I'm gonna need to know your real name."

This story continues in
Misadventures with a Country Boy!

ACKNOWLEDGMENTS

I want to express my heartfelt gratitude to Dr. Gary Lorden, Professor of Mathematics and brilliant mind, for so generously helping me get the math and gambling right in this story. Thank you also to Toby Wheeler, cybersecurity specialist, for helping me make Savvy a superheroine in as accurate and realistic a manner as possible. Thank you to the team at Waterhouse Press for your hard work and for making my entire Misadventures experience so wonderful. And, of course, thank you, dear reader, for reading this book!

MORE MISADVENTURES

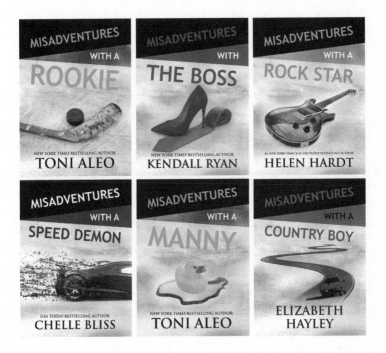

MISADVENTURES WITH A ROOKIE
NEW YORK TIMES BESTSELLING AUTHOR
TONI ALEO

MISADVENTURES WITH THE BOSS
NEW YORK TIMES BESTSELLING AUTHOR
KENDALL RYAN

MISADVENTURES WITH A ROCK STAR
#1 NEW YORK TIMES & #1 USA TODAY BESTSELLING AUTHOR
HELEN HARDT

MISADVENTURES WITH A SPEED DEMON
USA TODAY BESTSELLING AUTHOR
CHELLE BLISS

MISADVENTURES WITH A MANNY
NEW YORK TIMES BESTSELLING AUTHOR
TONI ALEO

MISADVENTURES WITH A COUNTRY BOY
ELIZABETH HAYLEY

VISIT MISADVENTURES.COM
FOR MORE INFORMATION!